the
mysterious
edge of the
heroic world

Also by E. L. Konigsburg

cഅ ഔ

the mysterious edge of the heroic world

e. l. konigsburg

ginee seo books
Atheneum Books for Young Readers
NEW YORK LONDON TORONTO SYDNEY

Atheneum Books for Young Readers
An imprint of Simon & Schuster Children's Publishing Division
1230 Avenue of the Americas
New York, New York 10020
"How to Tell Portraits from Still-Lifes," "On the Farther Wall, Marc
Chagall," "The Modern Palette," from *Times Three* by Phyllis McGinley,
copyright 1932–1960 by Phyllis McGinley; Copyright 1938–42, 1944,
1945, 1958, 1959 by The Curtis Publishing Co. Used by permission of
Viking Penguin, a division of Penguin Group (USA) Inc.
Book design by Mike Rosamilia
The text for this book is set in Bembo.
Manufactured in the United States of America
First Edition
2 4 6 8 10 9 7 5 3 1
CIP data for this book is available from the Library of Congress.
ISBN-13: 978-1-4169-4972-5
ISBN-10: 1-4169-4972-0

this **book** is for—

my **hands-on family**: ross adam **konigsburg**,
   sherry **berks**, michael **berks**, harriett **rosenberg**,
   leonard **rosenberg**, paul **konigsburg**,
   lesley **konigsburg**, laurie **todd**, robert **todd**;
and **friends**: joan **hill**, susana **urbina**, judy **jacobson**,
   helene **edwards**, judith viorst, joan **monsky**,
   phyllis lewis/lesley kirkwood, debby/jack **dreher**,
   jane condon/dan selhorst, jane **novak**,
   helene baker, mary carr **patton**;
and **doctors**: **steven buskirk, louis russo**;
and the **ineffable**: bobbi **yoffee**

—**without whom**

the
mysterious
edge of the
heroic world

1

In the late afternoon on the second Friday in September, Amedeo Kaplan stepped down from the school bus into a cloud of winged insects. He waved his hand in front of his face only to find that the flies silently landed on the back of his hand and stayed there. They didn't budge, and they didn't bite. They were as lazy as the afternoon. Amedeo looked closely. They were not lazy. They were preoccupied. They were coupling, mating on the wing, and when they landed, they stayed connected, end to end. They were shameless. He waved his hands and shook his arms, but nothing could interrupt them.

He stopped, unhooked his backpack, and laid it on the sidewalk. Fascinated by their silence and persistence, he knelt down to watch them. Close examination revealed an elongated body covered with black wings; end to end, they were no longer than half an inch. The heads were red, the size of a pin. There was a longer one and a

1

shorter one, and from what he remembered of nature studies, their size determined their sex—or vice versa.

The flies covered his arms like body hair. He started scraping them off and was startled to hear a voice behind him say, "Lovebugs."

He turned around and recognized William Wilcox.

William (!) Wilcox (!).

For the first time in his life Amedeo was dealing with being the new kid in school, the new kid in town, and finding out that neither made him special. Quite the opposite. Being new was generic at Lancaster Middle School. The school itself didn't start until sixth grade, so every single one of his fellow sixth graders was a new kid in school, and being new was also common because St. Malo was home to a lot of navy families, so for some of the kids at Lancaster Middle School, this was the third time they were the new kid in town. The navy seemed to move families to any town that had water nearby—a river, a lake, a pond, or even high humidity—so coming from a famous port city like New York added nothing to his interest quotient.

Amedeo was beginning to think that he had been conscripted into AA. Aloners Anonymous. No one at Lancaster Middle School knew or cared that he was new, that he was from New York, that he was Amedeo Kaplan.

But now William (!) Wilcox (!) had noticed him.

William Wilcox was anything but anonymous. He was not so much alone as aloof. In a school as variegated as an argyle sock, William Wilcox was not part of the pattern. Blond though he was, he was a dark thread on the edge. He was all edges. He had a self-assurance that inspired awe or fear or both.

Everyone seemed to know who William Wilcox was and that he had a story.

⁛ ⁛

Sometime after William Wilcox's father died, his mother got into the business of managing estate sales. She took charge of selling off the contents of houses of people who had died or who were moving or downsizing or had some other need to dispossess themselves of the things they owned. She was paid a commission on every item that was sold. It was a good business for someone like Mrs. Wilcox, who had no money to invest in inventory but who had the time and the talent to learn a trade. Mrs. Wilcox was fortunate that two antique dealers, Bertram Grover and Ray Porterfield, took her under their wings and started her on a career path.

From the start, William worked side by side with his mother.

In their first major estate sale, the Birchfields', Mrs.
Wilcox found a four-panel silk screen wrapped in an old
blanket in the back of a bedroom closet. It was slightly
faded but had no tears or stains, and she could tell immediately that it had been had painted a very long time ago.
She priced the screen reasonably at one hundred twenty-
five dollars but could not interest anyone in buying it.
Her instincts told her it was something fine, so when she
was finishing the sale and still couldn't find a buyer,
she deducted the full price from her sales commission and
took the screen home, put it up in front of the sofa in their
living room, and studied it. Each of the four panels told
part of the story of how women washed and wove silk. The
more she studied and researched, the more she became
convinced that the screen was not only very fine but rare.

On the weekend following the Birchfield sale, she and
William packed the screen into the family station wagon
and tried selling it to antique shops all over St. Malo.
When she could not interest anyone in buying it, she and
William took to the road, and on several consecutive
weekends, they stopped at antique shops in towns along
the interstate, both to the north and south of St. Malo.

They could not find a buyer.

Without his mother's knowing, William took photos of
the screen and secretly carried them with him when his

sixth-grade class took a spring trip to Washington, D.C. As his classmates were touring the National Air and Space Museum, William stole away to the Freer Gallery of Art, part of the Smithsonian that specializes in Asian art and antiquities.

Once there, William approached the receptionist's desk and asked to see the curator in charge of ancient Chinese art. The woman behind the desk asked, "Now, what business would you be having with the curator of Chinese art?" When William realized that the woman was not taking him seriously, he took out the photographs he had of the screen and lined them up at the edge of the desk so that they faced her. William could tell that the woman had no idea what she was seeing, let alone the value of it. She tried stalling him by saying that the curatorial staff was quite busy. William knew that he did not have much time before his sixth-grade class would miss him. He coolly assessed the situation: He was a sixth grader with no credentials, little time, and an enormous need. He squared his shoulders and thickened his Southern accent to heavy sweet cream and said, "Back to home, we have a expression, ma'am."

"What's that?" she asked.

"Why, back to home we always say that there's some folk who don't know that they're through the swinging doors of opportunity until they've got swat on their backside."

William waited.

It may have been because he returned each of her cold stares with cool dignity, or it may simply have been the quiet assurance in his voice coupled with his courtly manners that made it happen, but the receptionist picked up the phone and called the curator, a Mrs. Fortinbras.

William showed Mrs. Fortinbras the photographs, and Mrs. Fortinbras was not at all dismissive. She said that the photographs—crude as they were—made it difficult to tell enough about the screen. But they did show that it might be *interesting*. She suggested that William bring the screen itself to Washington so that she could arrange to have it examined by her staff.

When school was out for the summer, William convinced his mother to pack up the screen again and drive to Washington, D.C., and have Mrs. Fortinbras and her staff at the Freer give it a good look.

And they did take it there.

And Mrs. Fortinbras and her staff did examine it.

And Mrs. Fortinbras and her staff did recommend that the museum buy it.

And the museum did buy it.

For twenty thousand dollars.

When they got back to St. Malo, William called the

newspaper. The *Vindicator* printed William's story along with the pictures he had taken. The article appeared below the fold on the first page of the second section.

⌘ ⌘

William was now standing above Amedeo as he crouched over his backpack. Taking a minute to catch his breath, Amedeo examined the lovebugs on the back of his hand and asked, "Do they bite?" He had already witnessed that they did not.

"They're harmless," William said. "They don't sting or bite."

"Are they a Florida thing?"

"Southern."

"I haven't ever seen them before."

"They swarm twice a year. Spring and fall."

Amedeo pointed to one pair that had just landed on his arm. "Is that all they do?"

"From about ten in the morning until dusk." William raised his shoulder slowly and tilted his head slightly— like a conversational semicolon—before continuing. "The females live only two or three days. They die after their mating flight."

Amedeo laughed. "Way to go!"

William smiled.

Amedeo picked up his backpack and started walking with William.

"Do you live here?" Amedeo asked.

"No."

"Then why did you get off at my stop?"

William's smile faded. "I didn't know it was your stop. I thought it was a bus stop."

"I meant that I live here. So it's my stop."

"I'm not gonna take it away from you," William replied, and his smile disappeared.

They had reached the edge of Mrs. Zender's property. Without a whistle or a wave, William headed down the driveway.

Amedeo stopped to watch.

William lifted the back hatch of a station wagon that was parked at the bottom of Mrs. Zender's driveway. No one who lived on Mandarin Road owned a station wagon. Mrs. Zender drove a pink Thunderbird convertible: stick shift, whitewall tires, and a car horn that pealed out the first four notes of Beethoven's Fifth Symphony.

Amedeo watched as William removed a large brown paper bag from the back. It was not a Bloomingdale's Big Brown Bag, but a no-handles, flat-bottom brown bag from a grocery store. He could tell from the way William lifted it that the bag was definitely not empty. He carried the bag up to Mrs. Zender's front door and walked right in without ringing or knocking. He knew that he was being watched, but he did not once look back.

Amedeo waited until William closed the door behind him before he walked down the driveway himself.

Amedeo had been inside Mrs. Zender's house once. Two days after moving to St. Malo, they still didn't have a phone, and his mother had sent him next door to ask the lady of the house permission to use her phone to "light a fire" under them. *Them* being the phone enemy.

Amedeo's mother was an executive with Infinitel, an independent long-distance telephone company that was a competitor to Teletron, St. Malo's communications provider. To his mother, the telephone was as vital a connection as the muscle that connected her hand to her arm. If St. Malo already had had access to cell phones, she wouldn't be in this predicament, but then if St. Malo already had access to cell phones, they wouldn't be in St. Malo at all. The only thing neutralizing her indignation about not having a working phone was the embarrassment the local company was suffering at not being able to properly service one of their own. But on this morning there was also the pool man (whom she secretly believed to be the one who had cut the line) to deal with. She chose to wait for the pool man herself and to send Amedeo next door to deal with the phone. Amedeo had been happy to go.

A wide threshold of broken flagstones led to the front door of Mrs. Zender's house. There were no torn papers and dried leaves blowing up against a ripped screen door as in the opening credits of a horror movie. Her grounds were not littered with papers but with pinecones and needles, fallen Spanish moss, and big leathery sycamore leaves. Her lawn was cut but not manicured; her shrubs were not pruned, and except for the holes through the branches that the electric company made to protect the wires, her trees were wild. The paint on her front door was peeling. Her place looked shabby. Shabby in a genteel way, as if the people who lived there didn't have to keep up with the Joneses because they themselves *were* the Joneses.

Amedeo wiped a moustache of sweat from his upper lip with the sleeve of his T-shirt. Like a performer ready to go on stage, he stood on the threshold and took a long sip of the hot, moist gaseous matter that St. Malo called air. He lifted his hand to ring the bell.

The door swung wide, and the entire opening filled, top to bottom, with a sleeve. The sleeve of a silk kimono. "Yes?" the woman said, smiling. Her smile engaged her whole face. Her mouth opened high and wide; her nostrils flared, and her eyebrows lifted to meet a narrow margin of blond hair. Just beyond the hairline, her head was covered by a long, gauzy silk scarf—purple—that was tied in an elaborate knot below her left ear but was still long enough to hang to her waist. She wore three shades of eye shadow—one of which was purple—and heavy black mascara. Her lips were painted a bright crimson, which feathered above and below the line of her lips and left red runes on three of her front teeth.

It was nine o'clock in the morning.

Amedeo had never seen anyone dressed like that except when he was in an audience.

"Hello," he said. "My name is Amedeo Kaplan, and I would like permission to use your phone."

Mrs. Zender introduced herself and commented, "Amedeo. Lovely name."

"Thank you. People usually call me Deo."

"I won't," she said. "*Amedeo* is Italian for *Amadeus*, which means 'love of God.' It was Mozart's middle name."

"It was my grandfather's first name. I'm named for him."

"Lovely," she said, "lovely name, but how did you get here, Amedeo?"

"I walked."

"You walked? From where?"

"From next door."

"Oh," Mrs. Zender replied. "I didn't know there was a child."

"There definitely was. *Is.*"

"I didn't know."

"I was at camp."

"Music camp?" Mrs. Zender asked.

She smiled expectantly, waiting for an explanation. Fascinated, Amedeo watched her upper lip squeegee away one of the red runes. When he didn't answer, she told Amedeo to follow her, and with a sweep of sleeve, she pointed the way. The underarm seam of her kimono was split. Mrs. Zender was not a natural blonde.

As they traveled the distance of a long center hall, they passed two or three rooms so dark it was hard to tell where one ended and another began. Every window was covered with heavy drapes, which dropped from padded valances. The word *portière* from *Gone With the Wind* came to mind.

In several windows, the drapes had been shortened to accommodate a bulky window air conditioner that was noisily waging war with the heat and humidity. And losing. They passed a dining room large enough to be a ballroom. In the semilight, Amedeo could make out a *Phantom of the Opera* chandelier hanging over a table that looked long enough to seat the guest list at Buckingham Palace. Opposite the dining room was a room with a baby grand piano; its open lid reflected the few slits of light that pierced the parting of the drapes. The darkness and the drawn drapes added a dimension to the heat. It was August. It was St. Malo. It was hot. Hot, hot, hot.

But the thickness of the air carried the sound of music—opera—out of the rooms and transformed the hallway into a concert hall. Amedeo slowed down and cocked his head to listen.

Mrs. Zender said, "So you like my sound system."

"Definitely."

"One of a kind," she said, "Karl Eisenhuth himself installed it."

"Karl Eisenhuth? I'm sorry, I don't know him."

"Then I shall tell you. Karl Eisenhuth was the world's greatest acoustician. He had never before installed a sound system in a private home. He had done opera houses in Brno and Vienna and a symphony hall in Amsterdam. Mr. Zender, my late husband, contacted him and requested that he install a sound system here. Karl Eisenhuth asked Mr. Zender why he should bother with a private home in St. Malo, Florida, and Mr. Zender replied with three words: *Aida Lily Tull.* That was my professional name. Those three words, *Aida Lily Tull*, were reason enough."

Amedeo said, "I'm impressed." He was.

Mrs. Zender said, "I'm pleased that you are."

And for reasons he did not yet understand, Amedeo was pleased to have pleased.

Mrs. Zender swept her arm in the direction of the back of the house. The hallway was wide enough to allow them to walk side by side, but Mrs. Zender walked ahead. She was tall, and she was zaftig. Definitely zaftig. She was also majestic. She moved forward like a queen vessel plowing still waters. Her kimono corrugated as she moved. There was a thin stripe of purple that winked as it appeared and then disappeared in a fold of fabric at her waist.

Amedeo was wearing a short-sleeved T-shirt and shorts, but the air inside the house was as thick as motor oil, and perspiration soon coated his arms and legs and made his clothes stick like cuticle. Mrs. Zender seemed not to be sweating. Maybe she followed the dress code of the desert and insulated herself with layers of clothing. Arabs and motor oil had been in the news a lot lately.

The combination of heat, music, and the mesmerizing rock-and-roll of Mrs. Zender's hips made Amedeo worry about falling unconscious before reaching the door at the end of the hall. What were the names of clothes that desert people wore? *Burnoose . . . chador . . . chador.* His mother did not approve of chadors.

The rock-and-roll stopped when Mrs. Zender arrived at the door at the end of the hall. She waited for Amedeo to catch up, and then with a flutter of sleeve and a swirl of pattern, she lifted her right arm and pushed the door open. For a minute, she stood against the door, her arm stretched out like a semaphore, beckoning Amedeo to pass in front of her.

He walked into the kitchen, and Mrs. Zender quickly closed the door behind her.

The music stopped.

An air conditioner was propped into the kitchen window and was loudly battling the throbbing pulse of heat that bore into the room. Like his house, Mrs. Zender's faced east. By August, the afternoon sun was too high to make a direct hit on the kitchen windows, but was still strong enough to bounce off the river and push yellow bands of heat through each of the slats of the Venetian blinds.

The kitchen itself was a time capsule. The counters were edged in ribbed chrome and topped with pink patterned Formica that was peeling at the seams. Near the sink sat a set of metal cylinders labeled FLOUR, SUGAR, COFFEE. There was a toaster oven, but no microwave. The stove was the width of two regular stoves, eight burners, two regular ovens, and a warming oven. It was gleaming bright, clean, and obviously had not been used in a very long time. It would take courage to turn it on. Cold cereal and vichyssoise would be better menu choices.

On the countertop in the corner of the kitchen near the dining alcove, there was a small telephone. Turquoise. Rotary dial. Not touch-tone. Amedeo had seen people in the movies use a rotary phone, and he knew the phrase "dial a number," but he had never done it.

Mrs. Zender said, "That's a princess phone."

"Does it work?"

"Of course it works. Except for my cleaning service, which is not here today, everything in this house works."

Amedeo lifted the receiver. The part of the phone he held to his ear had yellowed from turquoise to a shade of institutional green.

Mrs. Zender sat at the kitchen table. Amedeo felt he was being watched. He turned to face the wall of cabinets.

The cabinets reached to the ceiling. It would take a ladder to reach the top shelves. The cabinet doors were glass, and Amedeo could see stacks and stacks of dishes and matching cups hanging from hooks. Behind other glass doors there were platoons of canned soups—mostly tomato—and a regiment of cereal boxes—mostly bran. Everything was orderly, but the dishes on the topmost shelves were dusty, and the stemware was cloudy, settled in rows like stalagmites.

Finally, he heard, "Your call may be monitored for quality assurance," and was told to listen carefully "to the following options." He realized that he could not exercise any of the "following options." He could hardly press one or two when there were no buttons to press. He held his hand over the mouthpiece and whispered, "I'm supposed to push one for English."

Mrs. Zender smiled wide. The last of the red runes had been washed away. "Do nothing," she said. "Just hang on. When you have a dial phone, they have to do the work for you." She threw her head back and laughed.

Amedeo didn't turn his back on her again.

As soon as the call was finished, they returned to the long, dark hall, where the heat and the music swallowed them. Mrs. Zender paused to say, "I suppose you put central air-conditioning into your place."

Amedeo hesitated. Until that moment, he had never thought of central air-conditioning as something a person put in. He thought it came with the walls and roof. "I suppose so," he said.

"Sissies," Mrs. Zender said. Then she laughed again. She had a musical laugh. "I chose a sound system over air-conditioning."

"But," Amedeo replied, "I think you're allowed to have both."

"No," she said crisply. "Karl Eisenhuth is as dead as my husband."

"Oh, I'm sorry."

"Yes, a pity. There never will be another sound system like this one."

Reluctantly, Amedeo left Mrs. Zender, her veils, her house.

Now, Amedeo watched William walk through that peeling, painted front door without stopping or knocking and enter Mrs. Zender's world of sound and shadow.

2

PETER VANDERWAAL WAS STAYING LATE AT THE OFFICE.
He was hoping to get a great deal accomplished in this
uninterrupted time after hours. He was clearing his
desk to start preparing for an important exhibition that
was coming to the Sheboygan Art Center. The show was
scheduled for the first weekend in November, and it
was already the second Friday in September. School had
started and museum activity always picked up with
the start of the school year. There was a lot of routine
museum business he wanted to get out of the way.

Like most people who consider themselves more creative than organized, Peter had allowed himself a generous
dose of self-satisfaction at having sorted his papers and laid
them out in (five) neat stacks on his desk.

The phone rang.

Peter would later tell people that he could tell by the
ring alone that it was an emergency.

And it was.

It was his mother.

His mother would never call him at the office unless there was an emergency. Her message was softly spoken, but urgent. His father, who had been on kidney dialysis for years, had taken a bad fall. He was in intensive care at the hospital. His condition was critical.

As soon as he hung up, Peter booked a flight to Epiphany, New York.

He checked his watch and knew that he had just enough time to get home, throw some clothes into an overnight bag, and call a cab to get him to the airport. If he packed lightly, he could carry his one bag as well as his briefcase onto the plane with him. He looked at the (five) stacks of papers on his desk and stuffed them into his briefcase, one at a time and in no particular order.

As he left his office Peter thought that efficiency and emergency have nothing in common except that they both begin with the letter *e*.

3

AMEDEO HESITATED BEFORE WALKING FARTHER DOWN THE driveway, but he was pulled toward the station wagon and the door beyond it.

He stopped at the station wagon and cleared the love-bugs from the window. They crumbled softly and smeared the glass. "Sorry," he said as he spit on a piece of notebook paper and wiped clean a sizable porthole. He saw a pile of towels, a pile of bedsheets, and twelve (he counted) heavy-looking large aluminum cooking pots that were darkened with pockmarks up to their handles.

Amedeo reluctantly turned away from the car and made his way to Mrs. Zender's front door. He raised his hand to ring the bell, lowered it, raised it, lowered it, raised it, and rang the bell.

The door swung wide, and a tiny woman—not Mrs. Zender—opened the door.

"You're not Mrs. Zender," he said.

"No, dear, I'm not. Would you like to speak to her?"

Before he could answer, he heard footsteps beating a staccato on the hallway floor. The hall carpet had been rolled. Lying against the back wall, end-on, it looked like an Escher drawing. "Please keep the door closed, Mrs. Wilcox. You'll let the lovebugs in." Then Mrs. Zender spotted Amedeo. "It's all right, Mrs. Wilcox. It's the boy from next door." Turning to Amedeo she asked, "Is your phone connected now?"

"Yes, thank you."

"Touch-tone?"

"It is."

"A pity," Mrs. Zender replied.

She turned to the woman beside her. "This is Amedeo Kaplan, my neighbor."

He was pleased that she remembered his name. It had been weeks.

Mrs. Wilcox stepped forward. "Amedeo? I'm Dora Ellen Wilcox, William's mother."

William emerged from the gloom of a back room. He was now dressed in worn jeans and an old T-shirt.

"So that makes you William Wilcox," Amedeo said.

William squinted before looking left and right with mock concentration. "I guess so," he said. "I don't see anyone else that name might could apply to."

Amedeo said, "My last name is not the same as my mother's. My mother uses her maiden name professionally."

"So how do you know my mother doesn't do the same? She's a professional too."

"I heard you just say that you don't see anyone else—"

Mrs. Zender interrupted. "If you two have a quarrel, please carry on with the door shut. It's lovebug season, Mrs. Wilcox. Close the door!"

Mrs. Wilcox took a quiet half step forward, just enough to shoulder herself between Mrs. Zender and the door. "Sorry, dear," she said as she closed the door, leaving William and Amedeo on one side and Mrs. Zender and herself on the other.

As soon as the door closed, Amedeo said, "I know another mother who does that."

"Does what?"

"Turns away anger."

"Your mother?"

"No, not my mother. My mother is more the outspoken type." Amedeo quickly added, "No, I was thinking of someone else's mother. Her name is Mrs. Vanderwaal. She's the mother of a guy I know. His name is Peter Vanderwaal. He's a grown-up. Actually, he's a friend of my father's." William said nothing, and Amedeo felt compelled to continue. "Well, actually, I consider Peter Vanderwaal my friend too." William still said nothing, which made Amedeo speak with greater urgency. "Peter Vanderwaal is definitely my friend. It's his mother, Mrs. Vanderwaal, I was referring to."

Then William asked, "How do you know my mother does that?"

Amedeo swallowed. "Does what?"

"Turns away anger. How do you know that?"

"She calls everyone 'dear.' Just like Mrs. Vanderwaal, Peter's mother."

"Yeah," William said. He smiled. This time, it was an open smile, congratulatory, like a horseshoe of roses. "Yeah, Ma does that. It's part of her nature, and it's good for her profession."

"What is your mother's profession, anyway?"

"She's a liquidator."

"Mrs. Vanderwaal, the other mother I was talking about, is the mother of my godfather. Peter Vanderwaal. He's a godfather. A real godfather. Actually, he's *my* godfather. And we're friends." Nervous that he had inadvertently given offense, Amedeo persevered. "Peter is my godfather *and* a friend. Or a *friend* and a godfather. Whichever way you look at it, he's both. Mostly friend, though."

William smiled a half-measure. "I guess you think that

because my ma's a liquidator, you'll find a dead body under that stuff in the station wagon?"

"Will I?"

"My ma's the kind of liquidator who helps people settle their affairs."

Amedeo said, "And is that supposed to be less scary?"

William laughed. He got the joke, and Amedeo felt a sense of pride and relief. "Actually," Amedeo said, "my godfather, Peter Vanderwaal, is probably settling some affairs right now. His father just died, and he is with his mother, helping her. Did someone at Mrs. Zender's die?"

"No. Mrs. Zender's going to Waldorf Court."

"I guess Waldorf Court would be a place to settle affairs. Is that something like family court?"

"Waldorf Court is a retirement community." William hesitated and then added, "She's moving there. I guess you noticed, she's right cranky about it."

Amedeo nodded. "Cranky. Definitely cranky."

"Ma will calm her down."

"Yeah, like Mrs. Vanderwaal. I guess everything will be all right." Amedeo started to leave, but he didn't really want to. He pointed to the station wagon. "So I guess all that stuff is going to Waldorf Court."

"That's the stuff Mrs. Zender's donating to Emerson House."

"Emerson House? Is that the local Goodwill?"

William hesitated again. "No, it's . . . No. Emerson House is . . ." William took a deep breath before continuing. "Emerson House is a shelter for victims of domestic abuse. They have a thrift shop there, and that's where Ma carries the donated stuff. Even before she starts a house sale, Ma knows what will sell and how much the other stuff won't sell for. That way a client, like Mrs. Zender, can take it as a charity tax deduction."

"Like Goodwill."

"Yeah, like Goodwill. But Ma . . . likes Emerson House better."

"Because her client gets a better tax deduction?"

"No. No. The deduction is the same." William hesitated before repeating, "Ma just likes Emerson House better."

Amedeo knew there was more to the answer, and he knew it would be pushy of him to ask, but he did anyway. "Why?"

"It's the women. Ma cares a lot about those women. They get beat up at home, and they run away with nothing except the clothes they have on their backs. Sometimes they have kids with them. Emerson House hides them and then helps them start a new life. They get to shop at the thrift shop for free."

"How did you find out about Emerson House?"

William again didn't answer immediately. Amedeo waited. There was a history in this silence, but William was not yet ready to let it go. Finally, William answered a different question. "Ma found out about it a while ago."

William was holding back, but Amedeo didn't want the conversation to end. "So, like, what doesn't sell?" he asked.

Tilting his chin in the direction of the station wagon, William answered, "Old pockmarked aluminum cookware."

"What else?"

"Tablecloths that need to be ironed. Ironing boards. Ma thinks ironing boards will become artifacts of a pre-permanent-press civilization."

"What else?"

"Pressure cookers."

"What's a pressure cooker?"

"It's a heavy metal pot with a swivel top that locks. It uses steam under pressure and at a high temperature to cook food fast. They went out of style when microwaves came in."

And that is when Amedeo asked, "Can I help?"

"Nah," William said. "That won't be necessary. Ma'll have Mrs. Zender cheerful in no time. She can't stand anybody being mad, or hurt, or the least little bit upset.

Ma does turn away anger. Just like you said that Mrs. Vanderwaal does."

"Actually, what I meant was, can I help with the sorting and stuff?"

William asked, "Why would you want to do that?"

"I don't know," Amedeo said. "I just would."

William fanned a few lovebugs from the front of his face and then flicked off the ones that had landed on the back of his hand. He looked Amedeo straight in the eye and asked, "Does this kind of work interest you?"

Amedeo knew that this was not the time to tell William that he was longing to get back inside Mrs. Zender's house. Not yet. Not yet. So taking a cue from William's measured, guarded responses to all direct questions, he brushed lovebugs—real and imaginary—from his shoulders before answering, "Something about it must."

The boys stood on either side of a pool of expectation. Both wanted to wade in. Both hesitated. William said, "We don't have insurance." Amedeo waited. "Like if you get cut on glass or fall over something, we don't have insurance to cover you."

Amedeo said, "My mother has tons of insurance. My mother *believes* in insurance. We have insurance for everything. We have health insurance, life insurance, insurance for every body—human body, auto body." William

laughed out loud, and Amedeo felt a strange sense of victory. Something about William Wilcox made Amedeo
eager to please him.

William shrugged as if tipping his ear to an angel on his
shoulder. At last, with a flicker of a smile, he said, "I guess
you might could. Help, that is."

Amedeo didn't want to, but he knew he had to ask, "Do
you have to check with your mother?"

"Nah," William answered, and started to lift his shoulder
to his earlobe again, but stopped and squared his shoulders
instead. "Ma and me, we're partners."

"When can I start?"

"Soon's you change your clothes."

4

PETER VANDERWAAL'S FATHER REMAINED CONSCIOUS long enough for Peter to say his good-byes and to reassure his father that he need not worry about Mother; that he, Peter, was there, ready to help.

There were a lot of details to be taken care of. Besides arrangements for the funeral, there were piles of bureaucratic paperwork, but actually, there had been very little for Peter himself to do. His mother, Lelani (who had been born in Hawaii when her father was in the navy and whose first name never failed to lower people's expectations of her), had worked for the city of Epiphany for years. She was extremely efficient, and all the arrangements that needed to be made, had been. Two days after the funeral, Peter was able to book a return flight.

His mother knew that her son was anxious to get back. She knew that he had important work to do. He was director of the Sheboygan Art Center and had a major exhibit coming up.

But as he was leaving for the airport, she handed him a gray metal lockbox and asked him to take it back to Sheboygan with him.

"What is this?" he asked.

"An archive of your father's life. Take it, dear. It should go back to Wisconsin with you. On the plane."

Peter was dreading the two flights plus the hour-and-fifteen-minute layover in Detroit, and since he had carried on a briefcase in addition to his overnight bag, he would have to check his bag and be burdened with the care and keep of an awkward carry-on if he took the gray box. "Mother," he said kindly, "can't this wait? Please. Can't you bring it up with you when you come to the opening?"

"I would like you to take it with you, dear."

"Taking it will mean that I'll have to check my suitcase."

"Yes, dear." She held the box out to him.

Peter took the box from her and felt its heft. "How will this ever get through security?" he asked.

"That won't be a problem, dear. When they open it, they'll find nothing in there but papers. And the box will fit in the overhead or under your seat."

"I think this ought to wait until you come up for the opening of the new show." Peter knew his mother hated to "bother him with things," so he thought that his reluctance would be enough to make her reconsider. However, she was not to be put off.

"Take it with you, dear," she said. "I think you need to have it with you."

"I can provide archival storage if that's what you mean."

"That, too, dear. But more than that. I think you need what is in there."

"Need, Mother?"

"Yes, dear. Need."

Peter took the box.

5

AMEDEO CUT ACROSS THE GROUNDS BETWEEN HIS HOUSE
and Mrs. Zender's. He ran as fast as he could, but the
property was dense with live oaks and pines, so the soil
was spongy from fallen leaves and pine needles laid
down in descending degrees of decay. On Mrs. Zender's
side of the line, fallen branches and ropey kudzu vines
cluttered the way. On Amedeo's side, the path was clear.
The pines didn't branch for miles up, and the bark on
the long stilts of their trunks was loosely attached in
patches of a sloppy collage. The live oaks were as old as
history; their trunks were blotched with lichen, their
branches draped with Spanish moss. The lichen and the
moss were like baro-meters, inching from gray to
green—dry to wet—and the sunlight that came through
was refracted by air so moist it draped small rainbowed
droplets on the horizontal limbs.

Running across spongy earth to get home was new to

Amedeo. In his former life, he had always been a city child. He had ridden city buses to get to school and an elevator to get home.

Amedeo was a late-in-life child. His mother had had a whole life and a whole other marriage before he had come along. Her first marriage was short-lived and childless and she referred to it as "training wheels." Although Amedeo bore his father's surname, Kaplan, his mother continued to use not her first married name but her maiden name, Loretta Bevilaqua, professionally. His mother was an attorney by training, an executive by temperament. She described herself as a navigator. At work or home it was Loretta who determined direction, altitude, and speed. She was and always had been the principal breadwinner and decision maker in the family.

Jacob Kaplan—Jake—was the pretty one. He was an artist. Laid back and younger than his wife, he made a lot less money, so Jake was the family steward: He checked safety and offered comfort.

Being an only child and the sole passenger, Amedeo spent a lot of time in the company of adults, safely buckled in.

After her divorce from Jake, Infinitel offered Loretta Bevilaqua another promotion. This one involved relocating. Cell phones were on the cusp of becoming a major means of telephone communication, and Infinitel wanted Loretta Bevilaqua to transfer to Florida to buy land so that the company could build towers that would allow them to blanket the state with cell phone signals.

When Amedeo learned that his mother was moving them to Florida, he thought he would have to give up his major dream: to discover something.

He didn't expect to be a star explorer like Columbus or Magellan, men who set out with a mission and who had sponsors and whose names are as important as their discoveries. He simply wanted to find something that had been lost, something that people didn't even know was lost until it was found—by him.

When Amedeo was in the fourth grade, the owner of a farm near his mother's hometown of Epiphany, New York, was draining a swamp and discovered a mastodon tusk sticking out of the ground. The farmer immediately cordoned off the area and invited scholars from nearby Clarion State University to help with the excavation. By the time they finished, they had uncovered the complete skeleton of a fifteen-thousand-year-old mastodon. With that discovery only two hundred miles away, Amedeo wondered if any Ice Age wonders could be concealed beneath the skyscrapers of his hometown, New York City.

And that is when he joined the Backyard Explorers, an after-school club. There were not many backyards to explore in his neighborhood, but his group went on field trips to the American Museum of Natural History twice a year, and in between they learned about real backyard explorers.

Some of the stories involved boys who were not much older than he was. There was a famous true story of a young Bedouin shepherd who followed a stray goat into a cave in the Judean desert, where he found clay jars filled with ancient writings that turned out to be copies of the Bible that had not been seen for two thousand years. Those were the famous Dead Sea Scrolls. There was also the story of the four French boys who went for a walk one day and fell into a hole in the ground and found that the hole was the opening to a cave that had walls covered with paintings not seen for seventeen thousand years. That hole was the famous cave of Lascaux.

To find mysterious writings would be even more wonderful than finding a mastodon tusk, but when Amedeo learned that his mother was moving them to Florida, he thought he would have to give up his dream. What chance was there of discovering something in a state that has in its geographic center a Disney-designated Discovery Island that is itself in the middle of a designated Adventureland with a ticket booth at its entrance and a gift shop at its exit? What chance was there of discovering something in a state where every square inch of real estate has been explored and/or exploited or was soon to be purchased by his mother for cell phone towers?

Amedeo's mother explained that St. Malo was not Disney-Orlando, and it was not condo-Miami. St. Malo was in the north, in the part of Florida that had once been settled by the French. Amedeo decided that French was good.

And so was the place on Mandarin Road.

There were only two houses on their side of the street. Both properties reached from the river to the road, and the length of two football fields separated them. Built at the same time, the houses were fraternal twins. Theirs was Mediterranean, the other Italianate. Both houses had been built on the bank of a scenic curve of the St. Malo River, and the surrounding untamed natural wilderness kept them hidden from public view.

The grounds around their house were shabby. Worn-out, overgrown shabby. The driveway had broken chunks of concrete that had levered up like tectonic plates, and the lawn was a camouflage pattern of brown, black, and green: chinch bugs, fungus, and weeds. The house itself was hidden behind overgrown shrubs. Within the house, the walls were damp, and the floor warped. In one of the bedrooms, the mildew behind the wallpaper had seeped through in a mysterious pattern that Amedeo thought of as hieroglyphs. Cobwebs in the laundry room hung like hammocks, and even they had accumulated dust. The glass in the windows facing the river was as wavy as the lens of a cheap telescope and as pitted as a shower door.

The house stood close to the spot where the French had built a fort in the 1500s.

Amedeo remembered that it was a French soldier in Napoleon's army who found the Rosetta Stone while digging in an old fort in Egypt. And the boys who discovered the cave of Lascaux were French.

St. Malo could be all right.

As soon as she bought the property, Loretta hired an array of architects, contractors, and interior designers, and for a full year their place on Mandarin Road became a construction site complete with not one but two portable toilets in the front yard.

By the time Amedeo and his mother moved in, every square foot of the lawn—front and back—was manicured. Every shrub was pruned, every tree coifed, and every corner of the house was endlessly decorated. The house sparkled. The pool, enlarged and retiled, sparkled too.

There were no sidewalks. Except for the occasional

UPS or FedEx truck, the neighborhood streets were empty. There was an occasional runner, but no one seemed to walk anywhere.

Theirs was a pristine, lovely house in a pristine, lonely neighborhood.

Maybe because St. Malo was flat instead of vertical, maybe because Mrs. Zender had been part of the neighborhood for a long time, or maybe because the neighbors whose houses sparkled—they all did—resented the fact that Mrs. Zender's house did not, people talked. Between the time Amedeo Kaplan used her turquoise princess dial-up phone and the time he stepped off the bus into a cloud of lovebugs, Amedeo had heard enough of Mrs. Zender's story to know he wanted to know more.

c◯ ◯v

Aida Lily Tull had once been the richest girl in town. Her father, Aloysius Harding Tull the Third, and his father before him, Aloysius Harding Tull the Second, had owned hundreds of acres of timberland all over north Florida and south Georgia. They also owned the paper mill. They were called the AlTulls, and until just after World War II, half the people in St. Malo worked for the AlTulls.

AlTull the Third married Vittoria de Capua. She was

39

from Italy. No one asked from where in Italy. It could have been Rome, or it could have been Rimini. It didn't matter. She was Italian, and she was beautiful, and she spoke three of the Romance languages. Rumors were started that she was a duchess. The rumors were never substantiated nor denied.

AlTull built the big house on the river for her. It was the biggest and fanciest, most up-to-date house in St. Malo, and Mrs. AlTull the Third soon became a town legend. She was extravagant. People whispered that she had the undersides of her shoes polished and couldn't abide sleeping on sheets that had been folded. Contour sheets had not yet been invented, so the maids would iron her sheets flat and carry them like a tarpaulin to the bed and tuck them in with hospital corners. But she was beautiful, and she spoke three Romance languages.

In St. Malo, Vittoria de Capua Tull *was* a duchess.

No one saw much of Aida Lily as she was growing up. She went to a private school in St. Malo for only a few years, and a chauffeur drove her there and back. After school she had private lessons—voice and piano and Italian—so she never played with other kids. It was the era of the notorious Lindbergh baby kidnapping, and Aida Lily's mother, the duchess, said that she was guarding her daughter for fear of kidnappers.

Aida Lily became a mystery; famous but hidden.

When Aida Lily was about ten, she was sent to boarding school in New England and spent her summers with the duchess in Europe until World War II put an end to leisure travel.

Meanwhile, AlTull was making a fortune. The mills were manufacturing corrugated cardboard for boxes, and during the war, everything from food rations to toilet paper needed a box. Plastic for packaging did not come in until after the war.

Aida Lily Tull graduated from boarding school, but she was never presented to St. Malo society even though generations of AlTull women had always been prime debutante material. Her mother was Italian, and it was rumored that the duchess once said that the *so-called* debutantes never did much besides entertain each other at luncheons of iced tea and avocado salad, and everyone in St. Malo knew that Vittoria de Capua Tull served wine at luncheons even if the guests were young and debutantes.

Without making her debut, Aida Lily went off to Rochester, New York, to train as an opera singer.

St. Malo society never lost interest in the duchess or the family Tull and several years after what would have been her debut, those three words, *Aida Lily Tull*, began to appear regularly in the newspaper. Every week the

Vindicator seemed to carry an article on the front page of the Features section about Aida Lily Tull. The newspaper always referred to her as *our local diva*.

Most of Aida Lily Tull's career in opera took place in Europe. After World War II, before rock-and-roll hit the charts, the continent had many small, first-rate companies, and towns no bigger than St. Malo had opera houses. Aida Lily Tull never made it to any of the famous opera houses like La Scala in Milan or the Garnier in Paris, but she had a solid career in the first row of the second section. She toured with excellent small companies in towns all over Germany, Austria, and Italy.

Then Aida Lily Tull married Mr. Zender and moved back to St. Malo and lived in the big house on Mandarin Road and news about *our local diva* stopped.

で℥ ℘ひ

Amedeo couldn't wait.

As soon as he changed his clothes, he would be back. He would once again be inside Mrs. Zender's pneumatic music-filled house.

He flung himself through his front door, skirted around the kitchen, and started toward his room. His mother, who was on the phone, quickly hung up and asked, "What's happened?"

Amedeo kept walking as he tried to explain that he had to change clothes because he was going over to Mrs. Zender's to help Mrs. Wilcox manage the sale of her estate.

"Whose estate?"

"Mrs. Zender's."

"I didn't know Mrs. Zender was moving. There isn't even a FOR SALE sign out front."

"She is definitely moving. The rugs are already rolled."

"Rolled rugs don't necessarily mean she is moving. She could be having them cleaned." Then his mother stopped, thought a minute, and said, "I've seen her place. Having them cleaned is not a possibility, is it?" Amedeo laughed, and his mother asked, "Where is she moving to?"

"Waldorf Court."

"And where is that?"

"I don't know where it is. It's some retirement home she's cranky about having to move to. There is a Mrs. Wilcox who is liquidating Mrs. Zender's estate, and her son, William, invited me to help with the sale."

"He invited you?"

"After I asked him to."

Amedeo's mother followed him into the bedroom. "I think I should meet this Mrs. Wilcox."

"I don't think you have to," he said as he pulled off his shirt. "She's nice. She's just like Mrs. Vanderwaal."

43

"Peter's mother?"

"Yeah. She calls everyone *dear*. William told me to change clothes, but I think it'll be all right to wear these jeans over there, don't you?"

"Yes," his mother answered. "What time will you be back?"

"I don't know. I think I'll be going over there every day for a while."

"Every day?"

"If you've seen Mrs. Zender's house, you know there is a lot to do." His mother hesitated. As much as he didn't want to take time to explain, Amedeo understood that after-school visits were not something she was used to. In New York, visits with kids had involved a lot of scheduling: drop-offs and pickups. Even after he was old enough to get to and from school without an escort, there had never been anything spontaneous about his after-school friendships.

Amedeo pleaded, "Mother, this is something I definitely want to do. It's like Backyard Explorers. It will keep me busy after school, and you won't have to rush home from work. I'll be fine. There's a phone over there if you need to get me. Mother, please."

After another moment's thought, his mother said okay, and Amedeo was out the door.

He went around back and knocked on the kitchen door.
William called, "It's open."

And Amedeo said, "Yes!" and to himself he added
another *Yes!*

William was on a ladder reaching into the top shelf of one
of the cupboards. "It'll be a big help if I can hand you this
stuff and not have to climb back down the ladder with
each armful."

"Where shall I put them?"

"On the countertops, the table, the stove—on any sur-
face that doesn't wobble."

William waited patiently until Amedeo had safely
placed and balanced whatever had been handed to him
before turning back to the cabinet he was emptying. There
was so much stuff—so much—that it didn't take long for
all the surfaces to be covered with stacks of dishes and
cups on saucers. Amedeo asked, "What shall I do now?"

"Consolidate. Stack all the dinner plates on top a one
another if they're the same pattern. Same with the saucers
and so forth. Then make some nests with the cups. Soon's
we get these top shelves empty, I'll come down and help."

Amedeo waited until they were both at ground level
and had empty hands before asking.

"How did Mrs. Zender find your mother?"

"The Yellow Pages."

William sat down on the second rung from the bottom of the ladder. His legs were so long that even sitting on the second step his knees were steeply bent. William had started what Amedeo would soon learn was one of his customary long pauses when Mrs. Zender burst through the swinging door of the kitchen. "It's extremely warm today," she said. "I'm keeping a bottle of champagne cooling in the refrigerator."

She handed William her empty champagne flute, and without further instructions he went to the refrigerator and filled her glass. Mrs. Zender took it but didn't leave. She asked Amedeo, "Do you know that the famous Yellow Pages do not have an index?"

She had been listening.

"No," Amedeo answered. "I've never used the Yellow Pages myself. Sometimes my mother would look up the phone number of a restaurant, but she never used them for anything important."

Mrs. Zender said, "In my considerable experience, the phone number of a restaurant is not unimportant. Every conversation I have ever had in New York City either begins or ends with a discussion of real estate or restaurants." She lifted her glass but stopped it short of her lips.

"I was thankful that the categories are listed alphabetically." She raised high her arm holding her champagne and said, "I toast the good Lord for inventing the alphabet." She took a drink and added, "Although I am not certain He wants credit for what I found under the letter E. The good Lord"—she lifted her eyes and her glass toward the ceiling—"knows I am not a prude, but I was shocked at what I found there: **Errand Service**—RENT A WIFE: *Let Us Organize Your Space and Your Life.* And **Escort Service**—EXECUTIVE ESCORTS: *Major Credit Cards Accepted.* I say the world as it ought to be has come to an end."

Amedeo said, "My mother is an executive."

"Exactly!" Mrs. Zender said. "Executives are not what they used to be."

"Where in the Yellow Pages did you find Mrs. Wilcox?" Amedeo asked.

"Under the letter *E*," Mrs. Zender said, and swept out of the room, holding her champagne glass in one hand and pushing the door open with the other.

When the door had swung shut, William smiled shyly. "Ma is under *E* for **Estates—Appraisals & Sales**." He opened the drawer beneath the counter, where the turquoise princess phone rested. He took out the phone book and leafed through the pages before handing the opened book to Amedeo. Near the center of the page he pointed to a small boxed ad.

Dora Ellen Wilcox

Appraisals and Estate Liquidation
International Society of Appraisers

William waited until he was sure that Amedeo had focused. "Ma's name rang a bell," he said. "That's what did it. The name *Dora Ellen Wilcox* did it. Mrs. Zender remembered an article in the St. Malo *Vindicator*."

Amedeo took the prompt. "What was the article about?"

William tipped his ear to the angel on his shoulder and told Amedeo the story of how his mother had sold a Chinese silk screen to the Freer Gallery.

Amedeo asked, "Do you mean that your mother found something that actually belongs in a museum?"

"Bought it. She bought it from the Birchfield estate. Then resold it."

"Was it very old?"

William nodded. "Hundreds of years old. About the time of Marco Polo."

"But she did discover it, didn't she?"

William shrugged. "It wasn't like she discovered something that had never existed before. And it wasn't really lost because no one was looking for it."

With relish, Amedeo told William about the four boys who discovered the cave of Lascaux. "You could say that it wasn't lost because no one was looking for it, but you could *also* say that all those drawings were lost from sight. For seventeen thousand years they were there, and no one knew it."

"How do you know that?" William asked. "It might could be that someone had seen them just a thousand years before and covered them up again. Just like someone might could have seen that screen at the Birchfields' and just covered it up and stashed it back in the closet."

"Those kids discovered something. Something special, and they knew it."

William said, "Ma knew the screen was something special."

"I call that a discovery," Amedeo insisted.

William remained modest about the part he had played in the sale of the screen, but he was eager to tell Amedeo about his mother. "Before taking it around, Ma studied on it a long time. She determined that the pictures were telling a story about washing silk and weaving it."

As Amedeo was saying, "Some experts now think that those cave drawings at Lascaux are a kind of writing that tells stories," the kitchen door swung open. A hand holding a champagne glass preceded Mrs. Zender into the room. She walked over to the refrigerator, opened the door, and started fanning the air from it toward her bosom. Speaking into the refrigerator, she said, "Louis Pasteur said that 'Chance only favors the prepared mind.'" She topped off her glass, turned, but continued to stand at the open refrigerator. "If one doesn't want to be more anonymous than his discovery, one must have a prepared mind. Of course, Pasteur did discover something. I think it was germs. But Pasteur really did *invent* something. A process. He got the whole thing—*pasteurized*—named after him. Not like Columbus, who discovered America and only got the capital of Ohio named after him. Of course, Columbus didn't invent anything. He didn't really even *discover* America. It was never lost."

William and Amedeo exchanged a look. How long had Mrs. Zender been eavesdropping?

Mrs. Zender bumped the refrigerator door closed with her behind and kept her back to it. "Sometime just last week—or maybe it was last year—a man in Siberia had a woolly mammoth named for him because he *discovered* a tusk sticking out of the ground." Holding her champagne glass, she pushed the kitchen door open with her elbow, and as she stood in the doorway, said,

"They brought in bulldozers and cut out a huge block of permafrost and carried it off somewhere. They expect to defrost it. With hair dryers," she added with a hoarse laugh. "They claim they're going to save its sperm. For what? I ask. For whom? I ask. Who wouldn't choose anonymity over giving his family name to generations of wide-bottomed, extinct hairy mammals?" She was out the door.

Amedeo waited until the door stopped swinging before he asked William, "Do you think that's true about the woolly mammoth?"

William tipped his shoulder to his ear. "Mrs. Zender knows more than she lets on."

Then Amedeo asked, "Do you think we might discover something here?"

"Might could. When Mrs. Zender called Ma she said that selling the contents of her house would be more prestigious than selling the Birchfields'."

"Why?"

"She said the reason is just three words."

Amedeo said, "Let me guess. Those three words were *Aida Lily Tull*."

William's blue eyes fastened on Amedeo. "Yeah," he said. "Yeah, those were the three words." Suddenly, William clapped the phone book shut, dropped it into the drawer with a thud, and pulled the ladder over to another set of cabinets. He stood at the foot of the ladder and held on to both rails. He spoke to the space framed by the rungs at eye level. "When Mrs. Zender and Ma first spoke, Mrs. Zender told Ma that she knew she had to downsize, but she hated the word as much as she hated having to do it. She told Ma to never use that word— *downsize*—or the words *condominium* or *condo* or *unit* in her presence."

"So why is she moving?"

"She just told you: The world as it ought to be has come to an end."

"Is she one of those televangelists who preaches that the end is near?"

William laughed. "Mrs. Zender is hardly a preacher, and she isn't saying the end of the world is near, she is saying that the world as it ought to be has already ended."

"When did it end?"

"When the last full-service gas station changed all its pumps to self-service."

It was Amedeo's turn to laugh. "Does she really believe that?"

"She might could. She drives that pink Thunderbird, you know. Stick shift. Whitewall tires. Spoke wheels. Classic. Everyone in town knows that car and who owns it, and Mrs. Zender said that pumping her own gas is undignified."

Amedeo had seen Mrs. Zender behind the wheel of that car. He had watched her backing out of her garage. Top down, she twisted around in the driver's seat, kept one hand on the wheel and an elbow on the horn, and never looked in the rearview mirror and never slowed down until she was at the end of her driveway. Then she stopped—paused, really—long enough to shift gears before zooming down Mandarin Road, scarves fluttering and squirrels scattering. He pictured her pulling into a gas station, assembling her scarves, wedging herself out of the bucket seat, dismounting, and stepping up to a pump. "That would be undignified," he said. "Definitely undignified."

But once he said it, Amedeo's own good sense told him that there was something more than having to pump her own gasoline that was making Mrs. Zender move to Waldorf Court, and one look at William told him that he was right. "What else?" he asked.

For an answer William walked to the far side of the room and opened the door of the butler's pantry. He signaled Amedeo to follow. William closed the narrow door that trapped them in the small, stuffy, closetlike space that was out of range of Mrs. Zender's eavesdropping.

Without comment, William crossed the tiny room and pulled open one of a column of shallow drawers at the end of the counter. "Look at this," he said, holding up an elaborately carved fork whose tines and handle were black with tarnish. William reached back in the drawer for a spoon and a knife that were equally tarnished. "These here are sterling silver. Antique. We'll polish them before we sell them because that's the way Ma does business. They're black because they haven't been polished in years because Mrs. Zender hasn't and won't."

"Why?"

"Because the world as it ought to be has come to an end."

"The world with full-service gas stations?"

"And people."

"People?"

"People to pump gas and polish the silver. Her world is supposed to have people to do things for her." William carefully returned the silverware to the drawer. "This place where we are standing in right now is called the butler's pantry. Mrs. Zender had a butler who took charge of the silver and food service and managed the other servants. Mrs. Zender had people, and she had people to manage people."

"Won't she have people at Waldorf Court?"

"She'll have *services*. Waldorf Court has housekeeping

and linen *service*. Meal service and complimentary transportation."

"Why isn't that like having people?" Amedeo asked.

William shook his head and thought a while before
asking, "You from New York *City*, or New York?"

"The city."

"In New York City, having a chauffeur is having people.
Having a doorman to call you a cab is having services.
When you have people, you don't have to share."

"Just so you'll know. We don't have a chauffeur or a
housekeeper. My mother hired a cleaning service. There's
four of them. They come to the house twice a week and
swarm all over it like lovebugs. Mother also hired a lawn
service—there's four of them—and a pool service; they're
two."

"All those services take their orders from the crew
boss, not your mother. Your mother knows how to
handle them, but"—in a much softer tone—"Mrs.
Zender doesn't."

"She'll have to deal with them at the Waldorf."

"Not directly. They have an on-site manager to do that
for her."

"Like our building superintendent. That was New
York." Then he added, "*City*."

William rubbed his hand over the peeling Formica on

the apron of the scarred old slop sink. He turned on one of the spigots and watched the water run into the rusty drain. Then, without turning off the water, he whispered into the bowl of the sink, "Mrs. Zender needs the money."

In his whole past life Amedeo had never heard anyone admit to needing money. People talked about *making* money (from smart investments) or *saving* money (on good buys), but no one ever talked about needing money. In his previous life, when people said something was expensive, it was to brag, not to complain. "What money?"

"The money she's gonna get from the stuff we sell."

"Why does she need that money? She has this whole big house."

"She needs the money from this estate sale to pay off the balance that she owes on Waldorf Court."

"But she doesn't want to live there."

"But her neighbors don't want her to live *here*." William looked away from Amedeo. "The people who live on Mandarin Road don't want her here."

"I do."

"That's funny," William said.

"Why is that funny?"

"It's funny because it was after your mother got your trees trimmed and the underbrush cleared, and then like all of a sudden Mrs. Zender's house is exposed, and everybody can see it's a shambles, and the neighbors decide it is dragging down their real estate values, and they form a Neighborhood Watch committee and sign a petition asking Mrs. Zender to clean her place up."

"So why doesn't she? She could fix this place up, put in air-conditioning, and stay right here. The house has good bones. That's what Mother said about our place."

"It's a Catch-22. To have enough money to fix up her house proper she will have to sell her house to have the money to fix it up."

"She could take out a loan from a bank. People in New York do it all the time. It's called a mortgage."

"I *know* what it's called," William said. He bit the inside of his lower lip and added, "Rich kids like you don't get it."

That line fell like a plumb stone between them.

Amedeo's heart stopped. Maybe because he had never before been singled out as rich, maybe because William had said rich kids *like you*, or maybe because of the way he had said it, the pantry had become a bell jar, hot and silent, with the two of them both inside and outside—watching and being watched. Amedeo didn't know what to say or even if he should say anything. He waited, aching with disappointment.

"Taking out a mortgage is something Aida Lily Tull

would never do. A mortgage would put her in the same category as you and her other neighbors. Middle class."

Amedeo asked heatedly, "So which am I? Rich or middle class?"

William thought a long time before saying, "Both."

"And what is Mrs. Zender?"

"Was rich a while back. Never had a mortgage. Never was middle class."

That pushed Amedeo over the line, and he raised his voice. "I don't know if I'm rich or middle class, or if I have a mortgage, but"—William made no attempt to hush him—"I don't think any of those things make me mean or selfish, and they don't make you the Good Humor man either."

After a tilt of his head to the angel on his shoulder, William asked, "Would you want to borrow money to live in a neighborhood where no one wants you?"

"You just better watch who you call *no one*. I am not no one." Amedeo was almost shouting. He didn't care that—and perhaps even wanted—what he had to say would leave the butler's pantry and carry through walls all the way to Mrs. Zender, who at this minute might be listening at the kitchen door. "I am Amedeo Kaplan," he declared, "and I, Amedeo Kaplan, *am and want to be* Mrs. Zender's neighbor."

Without another word, William walked out of the butler's pantry. He left the door open, and Amedeo called after him, "I'll tell you one more thing, William Wilcox. Whatever I am—rich or middle class or whatever—I am not a snob about it. I have respect for people who mow their own lawns, and who clean their own silverware, and I am not like some other people in this room who are in awe of people who have people."

Through the open door, Amedeo watched a silent and stiff-necked William pull the ladder over to the next set of cabinets and climb up. He waited until William pulled out a stack of dishes.

Speaking to the dusty recesses of the top shelf, William asked, "Do you still want to work here?"

"How soon do you need to know?"

"As soon as I find out whether I'll be handing these dishes over to you or whether I'll be coming down this ladder with them."

For an answer, Amedeo walked through the pantry door, reached up, and took the dishes.

6

PETER VANDERWAAL WAS STUCK IN THE DETROIT AIRPORT.
The second of the two flights that would take him back
to Sheboygan was delayed. He set the metal lockbox on
the torn leatherette seat next to him, but as he waited,
more delays were announced, and the waiting area filled
up. Peter's conscience would not allow the metal box to
take up one of the last available seats, so he picked it up
to place it on the floor. As he lifted it over the arm of
the chair, the lid opened—he had forgotten to lock the
box after going through security. The papers tilted and
crept up toward the opening. He stood up to have better
leverage in balancing the contents, and as he reshuffled
the pages to make them lie flat, he felt a metal divider,
loosely fitted on the bottom. Impatient to realign the
papers back inside the box, he sat down and put the
box on his lap. He lifted the panel and found a pad of
yellow lined paper underneath. The pages were foxed,

the edges darkened. Peter recognized his father's hand-writing. The first page said:

THE STORY OF A LIFE, MINE
Written from Memory
by John Vanderwaal

Peter held on to the tablet and wedged the box between his feet. As he started to read, he found himself tightening his hold on the box with his ankles. The story began.

Before the war I was born at home in the city of Amsterdam, Holland. I was the second child born to Hubert and Isabellen van der Waal who were my parents. I came late to them, a surprise. When I was born, my older brother, Pieter, was already a grown man.

Following my birth, I had some good fortunes and some bad.

The bad fortune was that my mother and my father died when I was eight years of age. The good fortune was that I had a brother, Pieter, who loved me, and who took me to live with him. My brother, Pieter, was not married. This was in the year 1937.

I had happy years living with my brother, Pieter.

He owned a gallery for decorative arts on Prinsengracht where is now a hotel and which street farther up is famous for the Anne Frank Huis. In his shop Pieter sold furniture, mostly antiques, and other items to decorate your house, like Delft porcelains and minor paintings. Pieter lived over his shop as did many people in Amsterdam. My brother had two employees name of Gerard and Jacob, and he had also a manager, Klaus. Klaus lived with us in the rooms over the shop and became the boss whenever Pieter was to be out of the shop. I went to school from there, and when I returned after school, I helped also in Pieter's shop which was near to the Rijksmuseum where there are many famous works of art from painters of the seventeenth century like Rembrandt van Rijn, Jan Steen, Franz Hals, and Johannes Vermeer. Johannes was also my name when I was a Hollander. Now I am John.

Pieter had a workshop in the backside of his shop away from the canal. In this workshop he repaired pieces of furniture which sometimes required the work of a true craftsman which is what Pieter was as well as Klaus. Sometimes they made frames for customers to hang their art. Also, he and Klaus repaired frames.

It is now the year 1939, a very dangerous year. In this year, the Nazis attacked Poland which was the neighbor to Germany on the east. In Holland we were the neighbor to Germany on the west, and even though Holland said it was neutral, we knew you couldn't trust Adolf Hitler who was made chancellor of Germany, what he called Deutschland, before in the year 1933.

In the back of the workshop which was in back of the gallery, Pieter had another workshop which was secret. This I will call the back-back workshop. My job was in the back-back workshop.

Now I will tell of the secret work we did in the back-back workshop. This was to make crates. The secret crates were for the purpose of storing the famous works of Rembrandt van Rijn, Jan Steen, Franz Hals, and Johannes Vermeer. These secret crates were made to fit each work of art and to protect it. The crate must be fitted perfectly because rubbing can cause scratches, and the wood of the crate must be very dry but very strong, and where we used excelsior and straw to pad the edges, it must also be very dry because moist straw can cause mold, what you might call mildew. These crates we made were for the works of art to be taken to national air raid shelters near Zandvoort and Heemskirk and hidden from the Germans. For packing we had no plastic or Styrofoam for they were not yet invented.

My brother, Pieter, and his friends Klaus and Jacob

and Gerard and I as well, we worked in the back-back after business hours. Gerard was a photographer, and his job in the back-back room was to photograph the paintings before they were put into the crates. He had for these secret purposes a small darkroom that was hidden also. This is where Gerard developed his pictures. Sometimes Pieter's friends stayed all the night, but my brother Pieter would send me up to bed by midnight because in those years I was a schoolboy still.

In the year 1940, on May 10, Germany took occupation of the Netherlands without declaring war. Four days later, they bombed our city Rotterdam and destroyed it. Dutch forces surrendered on the day of May 15, 1940. Queen Wilhelmina and our royal family fled to London and our country became Occupied.

The whole time the Rijksmuseum stayed open but of course without those famous works of art which my brother had helped to move out in time. The director of the Rijksmuseum now filled in the empty spaces with minor works which he took out from storage.

The next bad year was 1942. Here comes now the story of how came I to America, and I became from Johannes to John and from the three words van der Waal, *I became one word* Vanderwaal, *like* van der Bilt

became Vanderbilt *and* Van Rosenfelt *became*
Roosevelt. *But never so rich or famous.*

The writing stopped in the middle of the page.

Peter hurriedly flipped to the end of the tablet. There
was nothing more. None of the other pages had been
written on. He folded the sheets back and laid the yellow
tablet on top of the other papers in the gray metal box.

He was closing the box when he glanced to the right
and left and saw that those seats had emptied. People were
boarding. He checked the gate assignment. It was his
flight. He hurriedly locked the box, rummaged in two
jacket pockets before finding his boarding pass, and dashed
across the waiting room. He presented his boarding pass
and put its stub in his mouth as he ran down the jetway
with his carry-on in one hand and the gray metal box in
the other. Right and left, they bumped against his thighs
and his reading glasses slid down his nose. By the time he
got to his seat, he was exhausted and haunted. His father
had briefly come back to life in that unfinished memoir.
He felt that he had lost him again.

7

AMEDEO ALWAYS GOT OFF THE BUS FIRST. WILLIAM FOL-
lowed, and by some unspoken agreement, they wouldn't
catch up with each other until they were well down the
block, and the bus was out of sight. They walked together to
the end of Mrs. Zender's driveway, said, "See ya," and
parted.

Before they would start their work, they shared a snack,
which Mrs. Wilcox had prepared. It seemed there was no
end to the work in the kitchen. The room was quiet
except for the sounds of their voices as they talked and
the groaning of the air conditioner. There was no music
inside the kitchen until Mrs. Zender pushed open the
door, and they would hear a slice of sound, sometimes
a measure and sometimes a melody—depending on how
much clothing had to follow her through the door.
Sometimes Mrs. Zender stayed long enough to drink a
glass and a refill of the champagne she kept chilled in the

refrigerator. Sometimes she stayed and talked; they were pleased and flattered when she did.

It was hot at the top of the ladder, and they took turns climbing up and handing down. They worked well together. William washed; Amedeo dried. Or Amedeo washed, William dried. They stacked and counted dishes. They polished silver and brass. William inspected. Amedeo inspected. They looked for cracks and chips in cheap coffee mugs and delicate champagne glasses. William had a china marking pen to circle any cracks or chips they found, and he used that same pen to mark prices on old Pyrex dishes and bake tins. William got to do all the marking.

With his china marking pen, William wrote 50¢ smack in the center of an old pie tin. He said, "Sometimes the kitchen is the most work and the least profitable of all the rooms in our sale."

Amedeo asked, "If these old pie tins are so much bother, wouldn't it definitely be better to donate them to that Emerson House?"

"We have to leave some stuff heaped up like this in the kitchen. Some liquidators leave all their stuff piled up, dusty and tarnished so that people can sort it out for theirselves and think they have found a prince among frogs."

"Isn't any of this stuff valuable?"

William used a customary long pause to walk over to a cabinet in the far corner of the room. On a shelf at eye level there was a pair of candlesticks. He very carefully removed one and handed it to Amedeo. "Turn it over," he said. "Look on the bottom. See that mark? See those crossed swords?" Amedeo nodded. "That's for Meissen. German. Valuable." He turned back to the cabinet. "This one has a match, and they're both in very good shape. Probably worth a whole lot." After Amedeo checked them out, William returned them to the cupboard. "Very valuable. We won't even begin to wash them until everything is cleared outta here. We'll hafta line the sink with towels.

"After we clean them up, Ma'll study them marks on the bottom. She'll study all them marks, not just the crossed swords. She'll study the big ones, the little ones, the blue ones—what color of blue they are—the ones that are pressed in. By the time she's done, she'll know the name of the person who painted them and the year they were painted and probably will even know if the painter took a bathroom break between painting one and then the other."

Amedeo laughed.

"These will probably be the first things that Bert and Ray will buy."

"Who are Bob and Ray?" Amedeo asked.

"*Bert* and Ray. Better remember those names. Bert and Ray."

"Who are they?"

"They're antique dealers. They have a shop over in the part of town called Huntington. They used to manage house sales themselves, and actually, they are the guys who got Ma started in the business. When they got too busy in their antique business and didn't want to spend their time managing house sales, they turned their calls over to Ma. Then after a while, people started calling Ma directly. Word-of-mouth recommendations. About then, Bert and Ray stopped doing house sales altogether, but they've kept up their contact with Ma. They like Ma to let them in first; that is, before the sale is open to the public."

"Will Bob and Ray get their things wholesale?" he asked.

"*Bert* and Ray," William corrected. He turned away, exasperated, but when he looked back, he saw that Amedeo was smiling.

William waited a second more, then said, "*Bert* and Ray will get a discount. All antique dealers like *Bert*"—here he smiled at the angel on his shoulder—"and Ray get what is called a 'professional discount.' As long as they have a dealer's license. When it comes to quality antiques, it's harder to buy them at a good price than to sell them, so that's why Bert and Ray want to get in before the sale is open to the public. Ma always lets them in first."

"Didn't she let Bert and Ray in first at the Birchfield sale when she found the Chinese silk screen?"

William interrupted a long silence to say, "'Course she did, but they didn't want any part of it."

⌒◦ ◦⌒

When Mrs. Wilcox told Bert and Ray that she thought the screen was "something good," they said that they wouldn't have it even if she gave it to them. Bert, who was an ex-Marine, said that when he was in the service, every other sailor who hit Hong Kong had brought home at least two.

When the Freer required that Mrs. Wilcox provide a written offer, proving that she had an authentic bid of twenty thousand dollars for the screen, Mrs. Wilcox called Bert and Ray and asked them to send her such an offer, written on their Huntington Antiques letterhead. Worried that they could possibly be made to honor such a bid, Bert and Ray were reluctant to do it. William took the phone from his mother, and with the same dignified determination that persuaded the receptionist at the Freer to call the curator and the same perseverance that persuaded the curator to look at his photos, William convinced Bert and Ray to send his mother a letter offering her twenty thousand dollars for the Chinese silk screen that they didn't want even if she had given it to them.

When the Freer Gallery purchased the screen and William called the *Vindicator* with the news, Mrs. Wilcox got many phone calls of congratulations from other dealers as well as from other people who had things they wanted her to sell. But for many days neither Bert nor Ray called. When finally they did, Mrs. Wilcox said, "I found out that that there screen was really worth twenty-five thousand. Guess I just still got a lot to learn."

When Bert and Ray teased Mrs. Wilcox about how she got "taken" by the Freer, Mrs. Wilcox laughed at herself right along with them.

That was her way.

Mrs. Wilcox had figured out that Bert and Ray were having a difficult time accepting the fact that she, Dora Ellen Wilcox, who had once been their student, already knew more than they did. And she had also figured out how to turn away their subconscious anger.

౸౸ ౷౺

"Bert and Ray can't but admit to theirselves that they made a mistake about that Chinese screen. But Ma is still grateful, so when she's doing a big sale like this one, she keeps a list of special stuff for them."

"Stuff like those candlesticks?"

"Yeah, they'll be right up there near the top of Ma's list. And in this business you also have to know *vintage*. Vintage means it's old, but not as old as *antique*. Like that big stove over there. Someone's gonna buy it. There's a big market for old bathroom stuff, too. Bathtubs with claw feet are very popular. And people even buy old toilets. That's because new toilets are made to *low flush* to save water, and sometimes, they just don't—flush, that is. But mostly people like these big old appliances. Appliances don't get to be old. They get to be *vintage*."

"You just said *old* kitchen stuff and *old* bathroom stuff, *old* toilets, and big *old* appliances."

"But to the customers we say *vintage*."

Amedeo repeated, "Vintage."

William motioned to Amedeo to follow him to the other side of the room. From the bottom cabinet of the center island, he pulled out a heavy, metal, domed object. It was covered with a thick layer of sticky dust. "Now, take this here waffle iron. It must be older than tooth-ache." He pulled the cord from the base and began to wind it into a figure eight. The cord resisted; it was thick as a garden hose and the black-and-yellow cotton insulation was stiff and dry; the plug that connected to the appliance was as big as a hockey puck, and the plug that went into the wall as big as a doorknob. "Somebody's going to want this old dinosaur of a waffle iron. They'll get it all rewired and have the neighbors over for a waffle brunch."

Amedeo looked at the waffle iron for a long time. He examined the oil drippings that had congealed like amber down its sides. Without saying a word, he went to the sink and wet a wad of paper towel. With it he rubbed enough grime from the top to make a small convex reflecting mirror. He said, "Maybe they will just put it on a tabletop and display it like a piece of Art Deco sculpture."

William laughed. "What do you know about Art Deco?"

Amedeo immediately answered, "The Chrysler Building in New York is Art Deco."

William coiled the last foot of the electric cord and pulled the plug through one of the loops, plunked it onto the countertop, and demanded, "What else?"

"I know that Art Deco was the style between World War I and World War II."

"How do you know all that?"

Amedeo said, "My dad is an artist. I know a lot about art. Jake—my dad—he mostly paints nudes, so I know that a nude is not the same thing as naked. Jake—my dad—has a lot of friends who are artists, and my god-father, Peter Vanderwaal, is an art director. I've definitely been to more art exhibits than most kids my age have been to movies."

William crossed his arms across his chest and said, "You have twenty-four seconds to list all the other talents you have."

Amedeo said, "Well, to start: I am a city child and a child of divorce."

"Seventeen seconds."

"My mother is an executive."

"Fourteen."

"I know what ASAP and *per diem* mean, and I know how to eat an artichoke."

William laughed out loud.

"Knowing how to eat an artichoke is definitely a skill not to be laughed at. When entertaining clients at a fine restaurant that may not be listed—even in small type in the Yellow Pages—you sometimes have to eat an artichoke, and if you are there with my executive mother, you better know how to get to the heart of an artichoke . . ."

"Or?"

"Or . . . you don't want to know."

"I do. I do want to know. Or what?"

"Or you better order collard greens."

"Nothing wrong with collard greens."

"Wouldn't know. Never had them."

"City child," William said and reached into his pocket, took out two china markers, and offered one to Amedeo. Amedeo took it as he would a baton in a relay.

8

THE FLIGHT TO SHEBOYGAN WAS SHORT AND BUMPY. PETER hardly knew if the pilot ever turned off the seat belt sign. As soon as he was buckled in and his briefcase stashed beneath the seat in front of him and the gray box securely placed in the overhead bin, he fell into a short, noisy, disordered sleep. Peter either snorted or snored through the announcement that they had reached cruising altitude and passengers were free to move about the cabin. He didn't care. He was too tired to move. He had a dim sense that the flight attendant had come by, but he would not have lifted his head had she been bringing champagne, caviar, and toast points instead of juice and pretzels. Peter missed the airline peanuts. He hated that they had switched to pretzels—peanuts optional. He stirred when he heard the wheeze of the wheels unlock, but he did not fully awaken until he heard, "Please return your seats to their full upright and locked positions." Peter had nothing to return. His seat as well as his reading glasses had been *full upright and locked* for the whole ride.

He left the plane and was halfway down the concourse before he remembered that he had checked his bag because he had carried on the gray box. He retraced his steps and waited at baggage claim. Like every other part of this journey, the wait was endless.

Peter Vanderwaal did not own a car and did not drive. He found a pay phone and called a taxi. He waited on the curb by Ground Transportation, so tired his toenails ached.

When he got to his apartment, he dropped his briefcase by his desk, wheeled his suitcase to the foot of his bed, and put the gray box in the corner of the closet in his spare room. He would break a lifelong habit and wait until morning to unpack. He showered and got into bed. He set the alarm for early the next morning.

He was up before the alarm went off and immediately unpacked. And then as soon as he dropped the lid on the hamper holding his soiled clothes, he shaved, dressed, and left for his office.

He would say later that as he slit the first envelope in the waiting mail, the fatigue and the pain of the past week consolidated into a neutrino that bounced around inside his head, firing up every circuit. The envelope contained the list of the thirty works of Modern art that had been selected for Sheboygan for the exhibition that he, Peter Vanderwaal, had been responsible for bringing to town. (Applause! Applause!)

Like most students of art history, Peter Vanderwaal knew some of the sad, twisted history of Modern art under Hitler's Third Reich, but he had never concentrated on it until he took a trip to San Francisco to see a collection called Degenerate "Art."

Peter had been fascinated by the art he saw there. He saw paintings by van Gogh and Renoir, and sculpture by Picasso. He saw drawings by Matisse. Some of the works were famous enough to have a place in the history of Modern art, but all of the works—*every* one of them—was famous because it had a place in political history as well, for every piece of art in the San Francisco exhibit of Degenerate art had once been stolen by an official member of a government.

The government was Nazi, the country was Germany, and the year was 1937, the year when Adolf Hitler erased the line between politics and art.

That was the summer when Hitler's propaganda minister, Joseph Goebbels, appointed a committee and gave it the authority to confiscate (read: *steal*) all those works of Modern art that it (read: *Hitler*) did not find acceptable. The committee stole over sixteen thousand works.

Six hundred and fifty of those stolen works were exhibited in an old warehouse in Munich in a show called *Entartete "Kunst."* Entartete means "degenerate," and Kunst means "art"; the quotation marks around the word "art" were deliberate. The purpose of the Degenerate "Art" exhibit in Munich was to educate the German people about the evils of Modern art.

The Degenerate art in San Francisco that Peter saw was a collection of one hundred and fifty of the original six hundred and fifty works that had been displayed in Germany in 1937, and it was that exhibit that opened Peter's eyes to how a dictator can condemn something that is new and different simply by labeling it evil.

The exhibit of Degenerate art traveled from San Francisco to Chicago and Washington, D.C. Record numbers attended, and everywhere it went, it raised the same questions: What gives a government the right to steal art? Who gives a government the right to dictate what people are permitted to like? How did it happen? Could it happen again? Should taste be a matter for a government to decide?

The original sponsors of the Degenerate "Art" exhibit wanted the dialogue to continue, so they made arrangements to divide up the hundred and fifty works into five sets of thirty and to send one set to each of five regional art centers throughout the country. People who did not have ready access to a major museum would then have an opportunity to see works of Modern art that changed the course of art and politics.

The regional art centers were to be chosen competitively.

Peter would later say that he had little hope of success when he wrote the application for Sheboygan.

When he got word that his art center had been chosen, Peter felt as if he had won the the Super Bowl, the Olympics, and the Powerball lottery. He was hailed as a town hero. (Thank you. Thank you very much.)

And now, on the very day he was back at work, he opened the envelope that told him that works by Picasso, Renoir, Matisse, and other major, major artists would be coming to town. (Applause! Applause!)

9

WHEN SHE HAD TO LIQUIDATE A LARGE ESTATE SUCH AS
Mrs. Zender's, Mrs. Wilcox took pictures of every room—
in whole and in parts—before she disassembled it. She did
this to account for everything in her sale and to help make
her lists. Most often Mrs. Wilcox's clients were heirs to the
place she was liquidating and other than the profit to be
made from the objects sold, the heirs had no interest in
the pictures she took.

But Mrs. Zender was different. Except for her frequent visits to the refrigerator and her occasional joining
in the conversation between William and Amedeo, Mrs.
Zender had no interest in the kitchen. But she insisted
on being in every one of the *before* pictures in each of the
other rooms.

Amedeo and William were often called upon to help
with the *mise-en-scènes*.

Preparations for the dining room photos were elaborate. Mrs. Zender selected an ostentatious array of china, crystal, and silver, all of which Amedeo and William were required to wash and polish. She carefully arranged them at one end of the long dining room table. Dressed in a haze of mauve chiffon and ropes of pearls and wearing—despite the heat—a plumed satin toque, she lifted a champagne flute in a toast to the empty Chippendale chair to her right. She then lip-synched the words of the drinking song from *La Traviata*, which was coming over her sound system. While Mrs. Wilcox patiently focused her camera, Mrs. Zender engaged in a long, hilarious conversation with the empty chair to her right and requested that Mrs. Wilcox keep her camera focused on her, not the empty chair.

Amedeo watched, fascinated. When they returned to their work, he said, "Mrs. Zender definitely loves having her picture taken."

"Maybe," William said. "Or maybe she just likes being center stage."

"I thought Mrs. Zender's whole career was center stage."

"The newspaper always referred to her as *our local diva*, but she mostly sang boys and bitches."

"Pardon me," Amedeo said, "but did you say *boys* and *bitches*?"

Amedeo had never before heard William Wilcox swear. His grammar sometimes slipped, and he sometimes used the *A* word, *ain't*, but his grammar, his shrugs, his silences were the personality equivalent of Mrs. Zender's unkempt grounds: There was no need to prove anything to anyone. He never used the *S* word or the *F* word. Not even a *damn* or *hell*.

"Yeah. Boys and bitches. That's what mezzo-sopranos sing. Aida Lily Tull was a mezzo-soprano. She sang boys and bitches."

"Excuse me, but did you just say *bitches* again?"

"I did," William replied. "Mezzo-sopranos have voices that are lower than regular sopranos, so they are given parts like Carmen in the opera *Carmen*. She's a bitch. Or sometimes mezzo-sopranos sing the parts of boys. When girls sing those boys' parts, they call them *breeches roles*. Like in one Mozart opera called *The Marriage of Figaro*, there is a part for a boy called Cherubino, which is always sung by a mezzo-soprano woman dressed up as a boy in Italian, even though Mozart was a Austrian."

"Why did Mrs. Zender stop singing?"

William shrugged. Not a one-shoulder shrug to his angel, but a two-shoulder I-don't-know kind.

"Come on. You must know. Or should I ask your mother?"

"Ma won't tell you. If she's got a client, she won't gossip about that client."

"It can't be that terrible."

"It ain't, but Ma thinks telling is." William lowered his head and rubbed his forehead. When he looked up, he said, "Ma thinks gossiping about a person gives a part of that person away."

Amedeo said, "I think you always give a piece of yourself away when you make a friend."

"But it's yours to give. Mrs. Zender is a client."

"But I think she wants to be a friend, too."

William had many silences, just as he had many shrugs. Sometimes he entered a silence as if it were another language, and Amedeo would have to wait. This one was a silence from which William emerged slowly. When he did, he said, "The stories in the *Vindicator* tapered off. Then the stories stopped. The stories stopped altogether until Aida Lily Tull's daddy died. Aida Lily comes on home to St. Malo for her daddy's funeral, and there is her picture in the paper. There she is right alongside her glamorous mother, the duchess. And there in the picture Aida Lily Tull is big. She is downright fat. Everyone in St. Malo figures that maybe she's not so big in the Europe opera scene anymore because she's got too big for her breeches."

"You mean that?" Amedeo asked. "Or you just trying to be funny?"

William said, "Both," and bit the inside of his lower lip to hold back his smile.

"So that was the end of her career altogether?"

"Probably. After her daddy is buried, Aida Lily goes on back to Europe. No one knows if she continued with her career after that, and if she did, it would've been brief, because within the year, she returned to St. Malo as Mrs. Walter Zender. Mr. Walter Zender, he comes back along with her. The two of them moved right in here, living with the duchess, and this is where Mrs. Zender has lived ever since—even after her mother died and even after her husband died too. I know she listens to a lot of opera, but I never heard her sing one note. Not even hum."

William said nothing more, but smiled at the angel on his shoulder.

When it was time to take the *before* pictures of the music room, Mrs. Zender insisted upon posing beside the baby grand piano. She wore her feathered satin toque, two long ropes of pearls, and white satin gloves that came to her elbow. "Watch your focus, Mrs. Wilcox," she cautioned. "I don't want the keyboard in the picture. There must not be even a hint that no one is playing." She tugged at her gloves and fingered her pearls. "You must not make me a cliché, Mrs. Wilcox."

Mrs. Wilcox took a step back and called, "Ready. One, two, three."

Mrs. Zender lifted her chin and opened her mouth. Her lower lip quivered as if she were delivering a note above the ledger lines. She held that pose for minutes while Mrs. Wilcox moved forward and back and took several more shots. After all the angles had been played, Mrs. Zender moved from the piano and started taking off her gloves. "I never felt more like myself than when I was on stage being someone else," she said.

"But," Amedeo said, "you were always a boy or a bitch."

"No, no, no," she answered. "I was *sometimes* a boy, and I was *often* a bitch"—she looked at Mrs. Wilcox and winked, and then she continued—"but what I *always* was, was superb."

Mrs. Zender decided to take the entire contents of her bedroom to the Waldorf. Every piece of furniture in that room was beautiful—elaborately carved, mirrored, or painted—and massive. Fitting all of it into a standard Waldorf Court master bedroom would be difficult, but size was not the issue.

The water bed was.

Mrs. Zender had one. Queen size.

Mrs. Zender insisted that she had slept in the finest beds in the finest bedrooms—and here she gave a wink to Mrs. Wilcox, which caused Mrs. Wilcox to blush—all over two continents, but her bed, the one she had here on Mandarin Road, was the only one that she had ever found that was not only comfortable but cool.

Mrs. Wilcox knew that water beds of any size were strictly forbidden in Waldorf Court, but Mrs. Zender chose not to believe her and insisted upon calling the property manager.

The property manager told Mrs. Zender that it was true—water beds were not allowed in Waldorf Court. He apologized for not having made it clear to her when she signed her contract, but the issue of water beds had never come up before.

—Why?

—Because no one here has one.

—I mean, why are they not permitted?

—Because of the damage they can do.

—My dear young man, damage may be done *in* one's bed, but not *by* one's bed.

—Mrs. Zender, water beds can leak.

—Don't be ridiculous. Pipes leak. Garden hoses leak. Even information can leak, but beds don't leak.

—But water beds do, Mrs. Zender. They can cause serious damage to floors and walls.

Mrs. Zender said that if she could not take her bed with her, she would break her contract.

The property manager said that he hoped she would reconsider. But water beds were strictly forbidden.

—No water beds. No exceptions. However, if you do choose to break your contract at this late date, there will be a financial penalty. That, too, is in the contract.

—Oh.

Mrs. Zender hung up abruptly, more agitated than Amedeo had ever seen her. Mrs. Wilcox immediately tried to calm her down. "There is a lovely four-poster in that guest room that faces the river," she said. "You might could take that bed instead."

"That bed is not queen size, and I am." Mrs. Zender pouted.

Mrs. Wilcox never argued and never attempted to override a veto. She went about her work, waiting for the hurricane force of Mrs. Zender's rage to pass.

"I would never have made that phone call, Mrs. Wilcox, if you had not brought the subject up in the first place. I could easily have taken my water bed to the Waldorf, and they would never have known. Now it will be the first thing they will look for."

Sensing that the worst was over, Mrs. Wilcox said, "They would have known, Mrs. Zender."

"How could they possibly have known, Mrs. Wilcox?"

"Your water bed would have to be drained before it could be moved. You would have had to refill it at the Waldorf, Mrs. Zender."

"Drained?"

"Yes, Mrs. Zender. Even if you was allowed to move it, you would have to drain it to move it."

"Drain it of what, Mrs. Wilcox?"

"Of water, Mrs. Zender."

"Is that what is sloshing around in there?"

"Yes, Mrs. Zender."

"Oh."

And that is when Mrs. Wilcox chose to tell Mrs. Zender that she knew a master carpenter who could adjust the bed frame of the lovely four-poster in the guest room that faced the river so that a queen size mattress would fit. A little later, when Mrs. Zender inquired about how one went about buying a mattress, Mrs. Wilcox did not tell her to look in the Yellow Pages. She passed her a list of stores that were well-known for courtesy and service.

The day following the water bed incident, Amedeo and William did their usual parting of the ways at the end of Mrs. Zender's drive, and Amedeo went home to do his usual hurried change of clothes. Amedeo's mother had come to trust his after-school project and often welcomed the opportunity to stay late at work. Amedeo was hardly inside his door when he heard the front doorbell ring.

There stood William, holding the bag in which he kept his change of clothes as well as the plastic bag containing the snack that Mrs. Wilcox always had for the boys to share before they started.

With a thrust of his chin in the direction of Mrs. Zender's, William said, "There's a situation over there."

"Do you know what it's about?"

"Telephones. Mrs. Zender found her princess phone won't work in the Waldorf."

"Can't it be retrofitted like the vintage appliances?"

"Probably, but I suspect that Mrs. Zender really wants new phones but wants to fuss about it. She is resisting. Ma says for me to change clothes over here and wait about half an hour before coming on back."

"Must be bad."

"It'll take time, and it won't be pretty. Ma will handle it, but she don't want me to witness her humbling herself that much."

Unlike Mrs. Zender's house, the front hall of Amedeo's house was not a passageway but was a wide, bright, open lobby that gave a spectacular view of the river straight ahead. The entire east side of the family room was a wall of windows. The room itself was two steps lower than the hallway. William stopped at the top step.

With a gesture he had learned from keeping company with adults, Amedeo beckoned William to have a seat and asked him if he would like something to drink. Still cradling his bag of clothes in his arms, William didn't move. He stood at the top step and looked around the room and then out the window at the landscaped terrace and the pool beyond. "I knew you were rich," he said.

Amedeo said, "I think we decided that that wouldn't keep us from being friends."

William set his bag of clothes on the floor before stepping down into the room. Amedeo went to the kitchen and returned with two cans of Coke, wrapped in paper napkins. Once seated, he placed a coaster on the table near William and asked him to help himself to the almonds that were in a clear crystal bowl.

William took a sip of Coke and carefully centered the

can on the coaster. He looked around the room. "My house is nothing like this. It's small, and it's in an old part of town. But it's beautiful. Ma has good taste."

Amedeo said, "My mother had a decorator. Decorators have good taste."

William started walking around. "Decorators like beige a lot, don't they?"

"Taupe," Amedeo replied. "Our place in New York was beige. This one is taupe, the daughter of beige."

"Taupe," William repeated.

Amedeo watched as William continued his survey of the room. He could tell that William hated what he was seeing. His house was too horizontal, too coordinated, too taupe. Too *done*. His house was too much a part of the neighborhood, too much a part of the Neighborhood Watch, and it made William feel that he wasn't. Amedeo pointed to a painting in the foyer. "Look at that," he said. "Not beige. Not taupe. My dad and Peter picked it out. They picked out all the art in our house."

William walked to the foyer and stood in front of the painting.

"That's an abstract," Amedeo said.

"I know what it is," William answered.

"Do you like it?"

"Is this some kind of test?"

"No. It's not."

"Is this something your dad did?"

"No. I just want to know if you like it. Simple."

"Well, I do. I like abstract."

Amedeo said, "Jake has taken me to see tons of abstracts. He told me to look at them like I am listening to a conversation in a foreign language."

William looked at him skeptically. "But don't you feel left out of the conversation?"

"Sometimes. Sometimes Jake and Peter—"

"Peter?"

"Peter Vanderwaal, my godfather. I already told you about him. He's director of the Art Center of Sheboygan. Peter and Jake would sometimes have a conversation about an abstract that took up more time than the artist took to paint it."

They walked back to the family room, and William asked, "Since you've seen so much art, what do you think of Mrs. Zender's?"

"Kitsch," Amedeo said.

"Kitsch?"

The paintings on Mrs. Zender's walls were modest landscapes framed in ornate gold frames and hung from silk cords suspended from carved ceiling moldings. The walls in the parlor were covered with red silk brocade, and the ceiling was high enough to accommodate two rows of paintings. Each frame had its own little light, which Mrs. Zender never turned on. "The light fades the brocade," she said.

"Maybe not kitsch. Maybe it's calendar art. Peter says that paintings of Elvis on velvet are kitsch and make him smile, but mediocre landscapes in elaborate gold frames are calendar art, and calendar art makes him want to cry."

William leaned back and stretched his arms and did a slow turn around the room. "Mrs. Zender told Ma that her husband bought most—or maybe even all—of the art for her house. She'll be keeping only a few pieces. To cover wall smudges, she said. And Ma, she's so smart that— without ever hearing what you just said—she turned on the lights that are on those gold frames, took a good look at each of the paintings, and said she's turning all of it over to an interior decorator and not even calling an art dealer."

When Amedeo and William thought that Mrs. Wilcox had safely turned away Mrs. Zender's anger, they walked over. Mrs. Zender approached Amedeo. "It seems I must purchase telephones. Since your mother is an executive with a communications company, I'll need you to come with me. We'll go tomorrow."

Amedeo was no more qualified than Mrs. Zender to buy a phone. His mother had always taken care of such things, and Amedeo himself had never set foot inside an office supply store or a large container store or even a Wal-Mart, but he wanted to do this, so he said, "Sure."

William smiled at him and muttered, "People."

For their trip to Dig-It-All to purchase telephones, Mrs. Zender wore a white linen pantsuit. Under the jacket she wore a purple beaded sleeveless blouse, and for a collar, she wore a pearl choker. Instead of her usual head scarf, she wore a headband of crushed pink velvet to which she had pinned a starburst of multicolored rhinestones.

They entered the store through an electronic scanner and were greeted by a young man dressed in black slacks and a red T-shirt bearing the Dig-It-All company logo. Mrs. Zender returned his greeting and then jumped back when he pulled a cart from a train and wheeled it to her. Both Amedeo and Mrs. Zender took the cart and started down a corridor, blinking into the blue fluorescence.

A woman wearing the same red T-shirt and black

slacks approached and asked Mrs. Zender if she could help. Mrs. Zender replied that yes, she could help by finding her a man who could assist in selecting a telephone for her new residence. "Yes," the young woman repeated, "how can I help?"

Mrs. Zender looked puzzled. "I thought I just said that you could find me a young man to help me select telephones."

"I can help," the young woman said. "I'll show you to Aisle Nine."

"Is there a young man in Aisle Nine?" Mrs. Zender asked.

The woman looked at Mrs. Zender. Up, then down. Up and down, before answering, "No, I am a woman. I'll show you to Aisle Nine."

"Shouldn't you be a man?"

"I don't think so," the young woman replied.

Mrs. Zender muttered, "The world as it ought to be has indeed come to an end."

"Come again?" the woman asked.

"Where? Come again where?"

"Please follow me."

"If I must."

Amedeo pretended that he heard nothing and followed the woman.

Mrs. Zender had to be reassured at least five times that having an answering machine would not be an invasion of privacy and demanded proof that the waves coming through a cordless phone would not give her a brain tumor. The salesperson had no proof, and Mrs. Zender lost patience before the saleswoman did. She turned to Amedeo and said, "Do you see that office chair over there?" Amedeo nodded. "I am going to sit in that chair and wait until you select a telephone for me."

Amedeo started to object, but Mrs. Zender said, "Do it," and she walked over to the chair and sat down. The saleswoman gave Amedeo a quizzical look that was an open invitation to comment on Mrs. Zender—her manner and her dress—but Amedeo pretended not to notice. People passed and stared, but Mrs. Zender sat with her elbows resting on the arms of the office chair and did not acknowledge their presence with even a glance, and Amedeo was pleased that she did not.

Amedeo tried out several samples and selected four. One for the living room with an answering machine; one for each of the bedrooms; and a cordless for the kitchen. He put them in the shopping cart, wheeled it over to Mrs. Zender, and instructed her to follow him to the checkout aisle.

"Four?" she asked. "Why did you get me four? I need

only two—my princess in the kitchen and an extension in my master bedroom. I don't need four telephones for the Waldorf." Then, as the clerk was ringing up the purchase, Mrs. Zender saw that one of the phones was cordless and another had an answering machine. "Why did you buy those?" she asked.

Amedeo opened his mouth in astonishment but said nothing.

The clerk stopped scanning the boxes and asked, "Do you want them or not?"

"Of course I want them," Mrs. Zender said. The clerk finished ringing them up, and Mrs. Zender presented her credit card. Amedeo was surprised she had one. She signed the sales slip with enough flourishes to make it suitable for framing.

Amedeo was neither pleased nor patient as he was made to wheel the cart toward the car. Mrs. Zender walked slowly behind. It was minutes before she caught up with him. He stood at the trunk of the pink Thunderbird and squinted, hoping his eyes were flashing thunderbolts in her direction. When she finally arrived, she reached into her purse for her keys and held them out to Amedeo. He knew he was supposed to take the keys from her and open the trunk, but he kept his hands wrapped around the handle of the cart. Mrs. Zender jiggled the keys. Amedeo pretended he didn't notice. She raised her hand so that the keys were right in front of his eyes, and she jiggled them again. Amedeo reached up and took them, unlocked the trunk, stacked the boxes in the trunk, slammed it shut, and walked around to the passenger side of the car.

Once inside the car—safety first—he fastened his seat belt. Then he crossed his arms across his chest and stared straight ahead, hoping the fire he was breathing would warp the windshield.

Mrs. Zender started the engine, and Amedeo shifted his gaze from the windshield to Mrs. Zender. She seemed totally unaware of his rage, so he erupted. Through clenched teeth, he said, "The point is you were right there in the store. You could have picked out what you wanted for yourself. You could have gotten off that chair and walked down aisle nine and seen for yourself what I had chosen. But no, you had to let me pick them out, and then you had to embarrass me in front of the girl at the checkout."

"I never thought I was an embarrassment to you."

"You weren't, but you made me feel like a dope in front of the cashier."

"That tells me you embarrassed yourself."

"You could have had the saleslady help you. You could have called your order in. Why did you bother to ask me in the first place? You didn't need me."

"I do need you." She glanced at Amedeo and then into the rearview mirror. "Let's not say anything more about telephones. They'll be fine, and so will you." And she backed out of her parking space and onto the road with what seemed like a single turn of the wheel. She shifted gears, cleared the lot, and zoomed down the street before saying, "Let's stop at the Dairy Queen, and I'll pick something out for you."

They were streets away from Dig-It-All before Amedeo had calmed down enough to say, "I have never been to the Dairy Queen. Must be Southern or suburban."

Mrs. Zender raised her eyebrows and smiled knowingly. "It's a drive-thru experience."

"Then it's definitely suburban."

Mrs. Zender expertly pulled into the drive-thru and spoke into a speaker encased in a large billboard, which displayed photographs of everything on the menu. Everything looked slightly blue. Mrs. Zender told Amedeo to trust her; she would order for both of them. She ordered two Peanut Buster Parfaits and drove around the billboard to a small window where a young woman handed her the order. Mrs. Zender paid, took the parfaits, and handed them over to Amedeo while she pulled the car around the corner of the building, parked, and turned off the engine. Amedeo studied his first Peanut Buster Parfait. It consisted of layers of frozen custard alternating with layers of peanuts embedded in hot fudge, topped with a mound of whipped cream and a cherry on top. Nothing was really blue: The chocolate was brown; the custard, cream-colored; and the cherry on top was red. The parfaits were presented in tall, domed, clear, cone-shaped plastic cups along with long red plastic spoons.

Amedeo watched Mrs. Zender plunge her spoon deep into the cup and bring up a geological layer of peanuts, fudge, custard, and whipped cream. She closed her eyes, leaned her head back, and licked her spoon. "Ahh!" she said. "Queen for a day." Opening her eyes to the sky, she added, "My mother is frowning down upon me right now."

"Your mother did not approve of Dairy Queen?"

"She did not." Mrs. Zender studied her parfait, scooped out another spoonful, licked her spoon clean, and swung it in the air like a conductor's baton. "Neither did Mr. Zender." She studied her parfait for the longest time. She fiddled with the spoon, mooshing the fudge sauce into

101

the custard. "Mother thought that if I were thin, I would be a better match for Mr. Zender. Mr. Zender was a thin man." She dipped the spoon back into the parfait. She polished off the rest of her custard, expertly scraping the plastic spoon along the inside of the container. She waited for Amedeo to finish before crushing her napkin and spoon into the now empty container. She handed them to Amedeo. He inserted one cup into the other and opened the car door, ready to throw them into the trash. Mrs. Zender said, "I want to tell you something." Amedeo pulled the car door shut. "After," she said. "After you throw that stuff away."

He hurried back to the car. Mrs. Zender said, "Fasten your seat belt."

"Is what you're going to tell me that shocking?"

She laughed. "Yes," she said. She checked the rearview mirror, looked around, and backed out of the parking space in one grand swoop, put the car into drive and swung onto the main road before she spoke again. "I was thin once," she said. "Does that shock you?"

"No."

"Good," she said, looking straight ahead. "But this is what I want to tell you. Ninety percent of who you are is invisible. If you weigh two hundred and fifty pounds instead of a hundred and fifty pounds, people are seeing twenty-five pounds instead of fifteen. They may think they are seeing more, but it is still only ten percent." She checked herself in the rearview mirror. "If I've done the math right."

"Did you ever weigh a hundred and fifty pounds?"

"I think I did once. What is that in stone?"

"Stone?"

"British stone?"

"How many pounds to a stone?" he asked.

"I think they do it in kilograms."

"It must be very complicated."

"Yes, it is," she said.

"And so is the ten percent that I see."

"Thank you," she replied.

10

FOR LONG HOURS PETER VANDERWAAL SAT AT HIS office desk writing copy for the catalog of the exhibit that would be coming to Sheboygan. He wanted the catalog to be informative and entertaining. He also wanted it to be a souvenir, a monograph, a historic treasure of a historic show that he, Peter (thank you, Peter), had brought to Sheboygan. But it must also provide guidelines (hands up, if you have a question) for the docents who would lead student tours through the exhibit.

He loved doing research. His kind of research was scholarly, sedentary, bookish. It gave him a chance to look up things that he had learned in school and meant never to forget—but had—and to look up other things that he knew would not be on the final exam but that he had always meant to look up when he had the time. The time (Applause! Applause!) had come.

For his introduction to the catalog, Peter wrote a brief history of the sad fate of the arts in Nazi Germany.

ɷ ɷ

Organized hatred of Modern art did not start in Germany until Hitler came to power. It started because Adolf Hitler had always wanted to be an artist, had not once but twice been denied admission to the Vienna Art Academy. The committee considered his sample drawings so boring that they did not even extend him an invitation to take the formal exam. Simply put, Hitler's art was not original, so when he came into political power, his resentment of the innovative, the creative, the unconventional grew and grew until he was determined to wipe Modern art off the cultural map of Germany. His war against Modern art started with words.

He declared all Modern art to be *degenerate*.

The Nazis plucked the word *degenerate* from a cauldron of myth and fear and loathing and distilled it into a politically correct reason for destroying Modern art. They used it over and over again like a battering ram.

The word *degenerate* itself was essentially a medical term to describe the condition of people who were not "normal" because of a nervous disorder. They defined *degenerate* as something so far removed from normal—so decadent—that it could no longer be recognized as belonging to the same species. The Nazis took pleasure in listing degenerates: Cripples, the mentally ill, Jews, homosexuals, Gypsies, Jehovah's Witnesses, and Bolsheviks were all by nature degenerates. All of them carried within themselves the seeds of a heritage, which was inferior to the natural superiority of the true German. Any work done by these degenerates was ipso facto degenerate: Any music they wrote or played, any building they designed or built, any painting, poetry, literature that came from their diseased hands or minds was diseased, degenerate, and as such was an insult—even a threat—to fine German feeling and intelligence.

According to Nazi theory, it followed that if the government allowed all of these inferior people—these mentally ill, these Jews and homosexuals, these Gypsies and Bolsheviks to live—they would procreate and produce a species that no longer belonged to Homo sapiens but to some lower, subhuman order, and eventually all German culture would degenerate. If these Modern artists were allowed to continue to produce their decadent, degenerate, insane art, they would be a grave threat to the natural superiority of German culture. To protect the art and refinement of the Aryan race all degenerates and degenerate work must be eliminated.

Just as the state had a responsibility to remove criminals from its borders, it must remove Modern artists, for Modern artists were criminals. They were criminals because their work was destroying German culture. Modern artists must no longer be permitted to work. They must not be permitted to paint, draw, or sculpt, and they must no longer be allowed to buy any of the materials with which they committed their crimes. Gestapo agents were given permission to visit the studios of those artists listed as degenerate, and if they smelled turpentine or found wet brushes, they had the right to arrest the artists on the spot.

In the summer of 1937, as a first measure in purging Germany of all existing Modern art, Joseph Goebbels, the Minister of Propaganda and Public Enlightenment, issued a decree that allowed his government agencies to seize all works of Degenerate art from public as well as private collections. Within three months, they had confiscated more than sixteen thousand works of art. Of those sixteen thousand, some were sold at auction, some were secretly given to Nazi officers, and some were burned as part of a fire drill in the courtyard of the Berlin Fire Station. And of those sixteen thousand works of art, six hundred and fifty were chosen to be displayed at the exhibit entitled *Entartete "Kunst."*

In the year 1937, on two consecutive days, two art exhibits opened in Munich, Germany.

On July 18, the Great German Art Exhibit opened in a newly completed state museum, the House of German Art.

With great pomp, Adolf Hitler himself presided over the inaugural ceremonies and gave the major speech. He started out by praising the architecture of the new building and trumpeting the important role that he, himself, had played in its design. Hitler went on to praise the art of the Third Reich by contrasting it with Modern art. And then he got to the meat of his message: Racially pure work was good and exalted the Aryan way of life; Modern art was insulting, distorted, and the work of inferior racial strains. By the time he got to saying that Modern art was destroying motherhood, heroism, and German culture, Hitler was wildly waving his arms and spraying saliva. He twisted around and thrashed about, and then in a power-possessed rage, he shrieked his real message: It was forbidden for artists to use anything but the forms seen in nature in their art. If they were either stupid enough or sick enough to defy his guidelines, if they continued to present "unfinished" work, if they continued to exalt the Jew and insult the Aryan, it would be up to the medical establishment and the criminal courts to stop them. "We will, from now on, lead an unrelenting war of purification, an unrelenting war of extermination, against the last elements that have displaced our Art."

By the time he finished, even his own staff worried that Hitler had gone mad.

The following day, July 19, 1937, in an old warehouse across the park, the exhibition called Degenerate "Art" opened. Six hundred fifty "racially impure, inferior works" of Modern art were crowded in nine small rooms. They were crammed together on the walls and floors. In an effort to make the work look ridiculous, some paintings were hung at strange angles. The walls were covered with cruel slogans painted in strong German blackhand. Young people were barred from attending because these six hundred and fifty works of Modern art were labeled pornographic.

Goebbels declared that the work was "such dreck that a three-hour visit makes one sick."

But people flocked to it. More than two million people came to see the Degenerate art—five times as many as came to see the Great German Art Exhibit. Curiosity brought some, patriotic disdain brought others, and despite the insulting slogans telling people why they should hate it, despite every rant of propaganda the Nazis waged against Modern art, some people discovered its power and (secretly) liked it.

◈ ◈

After finishing the first draft of his copy for the catalog, Peter Vanderwaal bundled the pages together, tapped all four edges until they were as tight and even as a Marine honor guard, clipped them together, and laid them tenderly in the center of his desk. He glanced again at the title page and smiled to himself as he read it: *Once Forbidden*. (Crisp! Elegant! Apt!) He congratulated himself on his choice and resisted the temptation to read again what he had written. He knew it would be better to leave it alone for now so that in the morning he would have a fresher look. He knew—absolutely!—that there could not possibly be a better title. (Applause! Applause!)

He left his office and paused just outside the door. The sun had already dropped and taken the day's heat with it. It was early October, and he could almost hear the leaves turning yellow. Peter stuck his tongue out ever so slightly—only slightly—so that he could taste the air. It was time: time to take his *pelzkeppe* out of storage.

Peter Vanderwaal had been in his twenties when he started losing his hair, so years before it became a fashion statement, Peter shaved his entire head. And long before it was common for men to do so, Peter had had each of his ears pierced: the right one twice; the left one, three times. His head shone like the moon, and his left ear twinkled like the bowl of the Big Dipper.

The winter after he took the job in Sheboygan, Peter commissioned a furrier to make him a tall, large, wide-brimmed hat that was a slightly scaled-down version of the one worn by the bridegroom in Jan van Eyck's famous painting *The Arnolfini Marriage*. It was his private homage to an artist and a painting he loved. In Sheboygan, Peter's hat had become more famous than the one in the painting that had inspired it. Peter's hat was known throughout the community as "Peter's *Pelzkeppe*"—Peter's Fur Hat.

Peter treasured his *pelzkeppe*. "It is the next best thing to having hair," he often said.

He bought two wig stands—one for his office and one for his house. Each had a place of honor on the far right corner of his desk, set out like a museum display.

Every year the children of Sheboygan had a contest. The first one to sight Peter's *pelzkeppe* called "Beaver! Beaver!" and if that child had an eyewitness, he or she won the right to sign his or her name and date on a small plastic statue of a beaver and keep it until the next first sighting.

Peter had known about the contest for years, but he pretended he didn't. On the day he first donned his *pelzkeppe*, he carefully mapped the route he would take from his apartment to the art center. He walked very slowly in the direction of the neighborhood of the child he currently believed to be worthy of the trophy. Despite the chill that came from his slow pace, he would not speed up until he heard the cry "Beaver! Beaver!" Peter was aware of two occasions when a parent rather than a child had done the first sighting. It was the same woman. It was late autumn, and both times she was waiting with her child at the school bus stop. Since he was not even supposed to know about the contest, he said nothing. But saying nothing didn't stop him from wanting to—even three "Beaver!"s later.

As he walked back to his apartment after having finished writing the copy for the catalog, Peter's thoughts turned to organizing all the activities that would be associated with Once Forbidden. (What a fine name.)

The exhibit itself was already a *cause célèbre*. The town fathers and business philanthropists had generously donated money to keep the museum open extra hours to accommodate the many classes that would take tours. His staff, too, was helping out. They had pledged hours of overtime to train docents who had volunteered to lead the tours.

To reward himself for the good work he had done that day, Peter allowed himself to fantasize about the grand opening party. It would take place the first weekend in November on the very cusp of the fall art and social season. It would be a gala occasion, but a formal one. He would wear his tuxedo—he loved to wear a tux—and he would request that all the male principals wear one too. He would ask all the women to dress very thirties-ish— as in 1937ish, to evoke the era of the original *Entartete "Kunst."* Three sponsors were underwriting the event. (Thank you very much.) He would engage the best caterer in town to provide the food, and a string quartet to play background music. There would be champagne, and he himself would supervise the design of the invitations. There was a calligrapher on his staff who promised to address them. He would personally select every bite of food and every piece of music, and he would invite everyone he knew, everyone from his personal and professional lives, going back to his grammar school days in Epiphany, New York.

Opening night would be a major—a *molto, molto*

magnifico—event. An event to go down in the history of Sheboygan. It would be *dazzling*!

By the time Peter unlocked the door to his apartment, he couldn't wait to start his list.

It was past midnight when he finished. He walked to the closet in his spare room to retrieve his *pelzkeppe*. As he reached for the big round box in which he stored it, he stubbed his toe on the gray metal box that held the archive of his father's life. He stooped down and moved the box farther back inside the closet.

He settled his *pelzkeppe* on the wig stand and returned its box to the shelf in his closet.

11

THE DAY THEY WERE SORTING OUT THE CONTENTS OF THE upstairs sitting room, the room that had once been Mr. Zender's study, Mrs. Zender sat in a red Bibendum chair and supervised their clearing out the drawers of a giant executive desk. Mrs. Zender said, "I am in no great hurry to move into the Waldorf."

Amedeo, who was sweating, said, "At least it's air-conditioned."

Mrs. Zender ignored him, and Mrs. Wilcox, forever worried that someone was offended, said, "I'm sure, Mrs. Zender, that you will be sorry to leave this house. It must hold a treasure of memories."

Mrs. Zender rolled her eyes. "There were parties, Mrs. Wilcox. There were many, many parties."

Mrs. Wilcox said, "I read about some of them parties in the *Vindicator.*"

Mrs. Zender said, "There were boating parties and tennis parties, and pool parties and lawn parties. I didn't boat, and I didn't play tennis, but I always dressed for the occasion. Dressing up has always been entertainment to me."

Mrs. Wilcox said, "To me and my family, reading about all the goings-on in the paper, this here house was like the court of Versailles."

Mrs. Zender protested, "Not Versailles." She thought a minute and said, "Sissinghurst. The only things missing from an English country weekend were the horses and the dogs. Mr. Zender couldn't ride, and Mother was allergic to dog dander. But there were plenty of dinner parties with white-glove service. And after-dinner drinks on the boat. There was one party when our crew took our guests down the river to Paloma. Everyone got off to be met by a fleet of cars that took them to a country barbeque place where Mr. Zender had arranged for take-out baskets of barbequed ribs and cornbread. Mr. Zender reigned over it all. The viceroy of Mandarin Road."

"Yes, I remember reading about that party. The *Vindicator* had pictures in the Sunday section."

"When we moved here after Daddy died, the house was already big enough for an embassy, but Mr. Zender insisted upon enlarging it. He added a dock and a boat-house at the end of the dock and a three-car garage with living quarters over it. The rooms over the garage were for 'our couple,' which was what Mr. Zender called the but-ler and cook." Mrs. Zender looked at Amedeo and said, "That's when we had people." She sighed and said, "The butler was Bridges, and his wife was Mrs. Bridges. Before Mr. Zender hired them, we had had a housekeeper named Jessie Mae who cooked, and a laundress who came twice a week. Bridges demoted Jessie Mae from housekeeper to cleaning lady and hired a cook. Jessie Mae quit. She called Bridges 'the Führer,' because he would never give her a lift to the city bus stop, which was a mile and a quarter up Mandarin Road back then."

"Still is," William said.

Mrs. Zender paid no attention.

"Jessie Mae was a proud cook, but Mrs. Bridges told Mr. Zender said there was too much fried food on Jessie Mae's menus and that the vegetables were overcooked. My mother, who was still alive at the time, agreed. Mother always had a problem with weight. My weight. But to me fried and overcooked are as Southern as marinara is Italian. I missed Jessie Mae's collard greens, cooked, over-cooked, with a *strick o' fat and a strick o' lean*, but the cook who Bridges hired made béchamel instead of gravy and said that collards are cow fodder."

"There's a lot of people who would say that," William said.

Amedeo said, "William knows that I prefer artichokes."

"Have you ever had collard greens—done right?"

"Never."

"I'll fix us some," Mrs. Wilcox said.

"And I'll open some champagne. Champagne and collard greens. Mr. Zender did not allow collard greens on our menu. He was a thin man."

"I remember from his pictures in the *Vindicator* that he was," Mrs. Wilcox said.

"Just before Jessie Mae quit, Mr. Zender called her into his study—this very room we're sitting in now—to talk to her about her attitude. Jessie Mae listened to everything he had to say, and then she said, 'Mr. Zender, you are one shallow man. If I gonna stick you with a toothpick, it gonna go right through you—front to back—and still have room to pop an olive on the end.' Then she untied her apron and dropped it on this very chair and walked out."

Mrs. Zender began to laugh, and William and Amedeo did too. Mrs. Wilcox smiled hesitantly before allowing herself to fully engage. Then Mrs. Zender added dreamily, "I missed Jessie Mae. I still do. But then, what could I have done?"

Mrs. Wilcox's lists were growing in number and complexity. One list was for the furniture and objects that Mrs. Zender wanted to keep for the Waldorf and her "shelf of her past." Those items were ticketed NFS—NOT FOR SALE—and tucked away in one of the guest bedrooms. A second list was for items that would be put up for general sale. She made a third list for special dealers who might be interested in large items like the paneling, the bathroom fixtures, or the cabinetry. The fourth list was for items that she wanted to recommend to Bert and Ray. They would be let in first, before she even advertised the sale.

The Bert and Ray list was the best. There were many fine family heirlooms, including some antebellum cabinet pieces, several superb sets of fireplace tools, an old mercury-backed mirror in a hand-carved frame, and a brass fender large enough to be the guardrail of the balcony in a small theater.

Preparing for the sale involved Mrs. Wilcox's examining the undersides of chairs, the insides of drawers, the bottoms of bowls and cups and saucers, always looking for clues as to their ages and makers. She sometimes sent Mrs. Zender searching through papers to find any record of when these purchases were made. The search was almost always fruitless, but going through her papers prompted an endless recital of stories.

Mrs. Wilcox was an apt listener. She enjoyed hearing tales of a life frosted with glamour, and Mrs. Zender needed someone who would not interrupt with stories that could possibly compete with hers.

The names Bert and Ray came up time and again, and the closest Amedeo ever heard William argue with his mother was when he heard him say, "Ma, they got eyes in their heads. They can see what all we got."

Mrs. Wilcox looked a little embarrassed and explained to Amedeo, "William don't feel as in thrall to Bert and Ray as I do."

William said, "Ma, you're even. You are out of debt, Ma."

"Well, William, we're out of debt because of them and the career they led me to."

"Right! And because of you they've made enough good buys to put them in a new income tax bracket. Ma, you don't have to be beholden to them anymore."

Mrs. Wilcox looked over her lists and did not reply.

William said, "Ma?"

"Yes, son?"

"Ma, did you hear what I just said?"

"Yes, dear."

"Well?"

"Well, that piano is gonna be a problem. It's so outta tune. Can't hardly keep a piano in tune with all this here heat and humidity. I think I gotta call in a regular piano dealer."

12

AFTER EXPLAINING HOW THE NAZIS HAD BEGUN THEIR CAM-
paign against Modern art by commandeering and corrupting
the word *degenerate*, Peter wrote brief biographies of each
of the artists to be represented in the Sheboygan exhibition
and why the Nazis thought each of them was degenerate.

୶୬ ୧ର

Henri Matisse: Degenerate because he was a member
of a group of artists called *Les Fauves*, which translated as the "Wild Beasts." Matisse dared to paint
oranges and apples in bold, flat colors that sometimes did not even hint at their natural shades, and at
other times he left whole sections of his canvas
unpainted. (Hitler had a particular distaste for any
work that he considered "unfinished.") What would
happen to German culture if it allowed itself to be
contaminated by Wild Beasts?

Pierre-Auguste Renoir: Degenerate because he was an Impressionist. He painted the way he did because he had a disease of the visual cortex, as did all the Impressionists. What would happen to German culture if it allowed itself to be contaminated by the work of people who were diseased?

Pablo Picasso: Degenerate because he drew inspiration from the tribal art of Africa. And what would happen to German culture if it allowed itself to be contaminated by the primitive aesthetics of the black subhumans of the Dark continent?

Vincent van Gogh: Degenerate because he was a diagnosed epileptic. He was crazy enough to cut off his own ear and give it to a prostitute. He had committed suicide, hadn't he? What would happen to German culture if it allowed itself to be contaminated by the work of crazy suicidal epileptics who cut off their own ears?

Marc Chagall: Degenerate because he was Jewish. The Jews—just by virtue of being Jews—by even a fraction of their heritage were the absolute worst contaminators of the Aryan race. What would happen to German culture if it allowed itself to be contaminated by Jews?

Georges Braque: Degenerate because he was a Cubist, a geometrician who painted in squares and triangles and scribbled dots and squiggles and wrote random letters and numbers on his canvases. His work did not deserve a frame. Braque was out of touch with reality. What would happen to German culture if it allowed itself to be contaminated by the work of men who lived in a fantasy world?

For the cover of the catalog, Peter chose to reproduce Picasso's *Harlequin at Rest*, a significant masterpiece from the artist's Blue period.

On the inside of the front cover, Peter selected a quotation by Goebbels that had appeared in the original 1937 catalog of *Entartete "Kunst"*:

> . . . the frightening and horrifying forms of the Exhibition of Degenerate art . . . [have] nothing at all to do with the suppression of artistic freedom and modern progress. On the contrary, the

botched works of art . . . and their creators are of yesterday and before yesterday. They are the senile representatives no longer to be taken seriously of a period we have intellectually and politically over-come.

On the inside of the back cover, he included another quotation—an epitaph:

Anybody who paints and sees a sky green and pastures blue ought to be sterilized.

—Adolf Hitler, 1937

13

Peter Vanderwaal slipped a note into the invitation he sent to Amedeo and his mother. The note read, "This show is major. The opening night party will be *molto, molto magnifico*—so glamorous that even Jake has promised to wear a tux. I pray that he has bought one. A rented tux is so father-of-the-bride. How do you like the title? If you tell me it's brilliant, I'll know that you are captive to truth and integrity. This is an offer you can't refuse." The note was signed, "Godfather."

As soon as the invitation came, Amedeo knew his mother wouldn't go.

Even though Loretta Bevilaqua had known Peter for a longer time than Jake had—Loretta and Peter had actually grown up on the same street in the same neighborhood— Jake and Peter were better friends. As adults all three had gone their separate ways until they joined forces to save from demolition three tall towers that had been built in the backyard of the house at 19 Schuyler Place. It was while working on the campaign to save the towers that Jake and Loretta met and fell in love.

After the towers had been safely moved to higher ground, they continued to require care and maintenance, and Jake was appointed their chief curator, so several times a year he traveled to Epiphany to check on them and do necessary repairs.

When Amedeo was little, and Loretta and Jake still loved each other, they used to make the trips to Epiphany together. Peter had often arranged to visit his mother at the same time. Peter loved the towers as much as Jake did, and he would accompany Jake on his tour of inspection, and then they would all gather at Mrs. Vanderwaal's house. Amedeo loved those visits with Peter and his mother.

After Jake and Loretta fell out of love and separated, Loretta stopped making the trips to Epiphany, but Amedeo continued to go along, and Peter continued meeting them there. Other than at camp and school, most of Amedeo's time was spent in the company of adults. None of Loretta's friends made a great effort to entertain him. Most often, he was relieved of having to say anything other than *please* and *thank you*, so those became his conversational necktie and jacket and allowed him to watch and learn the language of handshakes and air kisses. Loretta Bevilaqua said that learning to deal with boredom was the job of childhood and church, and only one of them was optional. Of all the adults that Amedeo spent time with, Peter and Jake were his favorites. They too allowed him to be a quiet observer, but he was relaxed and never bored when he was with them.

Jake was an artist, and most of his friends were artists. After the divorce, when Jake moved into the loft that he had been using as a studio, Amedeo split his weekends between his mother's apartment and his father's studio. There were no neckties and jackets in his father's company, and there he learned the language of bear hugs and smooches and high opinions loudly spoken.

Friendship takes up time, and Loretta was too efficient for it. Friendship is a combination of art and craft. The craft part is in knowing how to give and how to take. The art part is in knowing when, and the whole process only works when no one is keeping track.

Before he met William, Amedeo often felt more left out in the company of kids than in the company of adults, for his conversational necktie and jacket were inappropriate in one direction, and the loud, easy, sometimes profane talk among Jake's friends was equally inappropriate in the other. His friendship with William was there in the age-appropriate middle. It was there, and it was singular—well, one-on-one. It had all begun on the other side of Mrs. Zender's door, and without ever saying it, they both knew that what happened at Mrs. Zender's stayed at Mrs. Zender's. This friendship was Amedeo's, and it was William's, and it was theirs, and for as long as they could, they drew a thick black line around it and put up a NO TRESPASSING sign.

Loretta Bevilaqua knew how much Amedeo loved Peter, and she correctly guessed that he would not want to miss the grand opening of Once Forbidden. Amedeo correctly guessed that his mother would make arrangements that would allow him to go without her having to take the time to go herself.

Amedeo definitely wanted to go to the *molto, molto magnifico* party, but he also didn't want to miss out on anything at Mrs. Zender's—especially the library.

Mrs. Wilcox always saved the most difficult room for last. Usually, that was the dining room, where most families kept their heirloom silver and porcelain, but in Mrs. Zender's house, the library would be, hands down, the most difficult, and the library was the room they were now ready for. It was the one Amedeo wanted to do most, and it was the one he was going to miss, and his mother had already had his good navy blue suit dry-cleaned, pressed, and the sleeves let down, and she had already made reservations for him to fly as an unaccompanied minor to New York to meet Jake, and then travel with him to Sheboygan.

Amedeo waited until Friday to announce that he would have to miss work.

Mrs. Zender asked to see the invitation, and when Amedeo showed it to her, she commented, "Interesting title. What does it mean? Once Forbidden?"

She examined the invitation closely and read the inside fold several times. Peter had written: *Thirty works of Modern art selected from the original 1937 Degenerate "Art" exhibit in Munich, Germany.* "Do you know which artists' works you'll be seeing?" she asked.

Amedeo pointed to the front of the invitation. "There definitely will be a Picasso. Seeing a real Picasso will probably be a thrill for the kids in Sheboygan, but over the years I've probably seen more of Picasso than his wives and kids ever did."

Mrs. Zender read the name again. "Once Forbidden."

She smiled mischievously at Mrs. Wilcox and said, "I savor the forbidden. When Amedeo returns he will explain it all." She then announced that she too would be taking the weekend off. "I've scheduled a pedicure."

14

PETER VANDERWAAL LOVED BEING A HOST. OPENING NIGHTS were show business after all, and Peter loved show business, especially when he was writer, producer, and director, and had center stage all evening. He moved from one cluster of people to another, dispensing charm and accepting compliments like a film star at an awards show.

He watched a senior citizen point to an unpainted part of a canvas by Henri Matisse and listened to him ask a docent if the artist had run out of paint. The docent replied that no, parts of the canvas had been left bare on purpose to enrich the parts of the canvas that were painted. Peter smiled and mouthed *thank you* to the docent before moving on to a small group standing in front of Picasso's *Harlequin at Rest*.

Among them was a ten-year-old. There were not many children at the opening. Amedeo was the only one whose name had been written out on the envelope and the only one who had a name tag, which he had proudly stuck onto the lapel of the jacket of his good navy blue suit. The ten-year-old, like the others, had been vaguely included when the invitation was addressed to "So-and-So and Family." Peter had wanted this to be a grown-up event. The children would have their turn. As a matter of fact, they would have many turns. School tours were scheduled for every day of the week for the entire run of the exhibition.

The ten-year-old was standing only inches from Picasso's *Harlequin at Rest*, the painting Peter had chosen for the cover of his catalog. Hands in pockets, the boy rocked on his heels, exposing a strip of pink-buttoned belly flesh. Hardly black-tie appropriate.

Peter watched him rocking back and forth on his heels. Suddenly a giant pink bubble formed and grew on the boy's face.

Bubble gum!

Peter's rage exploded before the bubble did. He grabbed the kid's shoulder and pulled him back, away from the painting.

The bubble burst.

"What are you *doing*?" the kid asked, speaking through the thin rubbery film, which now covered his face from nose to chin.

e. l. konigsburg

"What are *you* doing?" Peter demanded in turn.

Mrs. Vanderwaal hurried over. "Is something the matter, dear?" she asked.

"This child was chewing gum." Peter could barely contain his rage.

Mrs. Vanderwaal said, "I know, dear, it's not good for the teeth."

The child's mother approached. She took her son by the shoulders and asked, "Are you all right?"

The child began peeling the burst bubble from his face. The boy's mother helped him peel off the last of it. She rolled the pink film between her thumb and forefinger. Peter watched, torn between fascination and disgust.

In that uncomfortable interval, Mrs. Vanderwaal turned to the mother and said, "My son was just so surprised to see a child chewing bubble gum. He had just mentioned to me that he thought that chewing gum among minors had become illegal—like smoking. He said he can't remember seeing a chewing gum commercial on television for years."

The mother said, "Your son obviously doesn't watch television at the right times."

Peter started to say something, but his mother interrupted. "Obviously," she said.

The boy's mother turned to Peter and said, "Nowhere is it posted that people are not to chew gum in here."

She took her son by the shoulders and led him across the gallery. As soon as they were out of earshot, Peter said, "Nowhere is it posted that you are not to chew gum in here, and nowhere is it posted that you are not to spit either. Whatever happened to the *unposted* laws of civilized behavior?"

Mrs. Vanderwaal placed her arm on Peter's elbow and guided him away from the Picasso. "Peter, dear," she said, "I think you overreacted."

Peter took a deep breath. "Really, Mother! Anyone who blows *pink* bubbles in front of a Picasso *Blue* painting should be arrested."

Peter would later say that he invited his mother, Amedeo, and Jake up to his apartment because any party as *molto, molto* as his deserved a second life. In other words, Peter needed more talk. They were no sooner inside the door than Peter loosened his cummerbund, removed his jacket and tie, and was again ready to take center stage.

Did they like the string quartet? YES.

And did you notice that the champagne was brut? YES.

And was served in real glasses. The stems always come off those plastic ones.

YES, the champagne was wonderful, and YES the champagne glasses were elegant.

Yes, yes, and yes.

Mrs. Vanderwaal said, "You are to be congratulated, dear. The evening was a resounding success."

"I know it was, Mother, and do you know how I know?"

"I wouldn't presume to know, dear."

"Well, the average time spent in front of a single work of Modern art is less than forty-five seconds. Doesn't that shock you?"

"Just a little."

"Of course, those are average times for average viewers, and that crowd this evening was hardly average. Do you know how much time some of those people spent in front of a single work this evening?"

"I wouldn't presume to know, dear."

"One couple spent so much time in front of the large Braque, I thought they might have taken root. They were mesmerized."

"I'm very proud of you, dear. Opening night was a resounding success."

Jake said, "A *molto, molto magnifico* success."

But they had to agree several more times. Too much praise was almost enough.

About midnight, Mrs. Vanderwaal excused herself and left the room. Everyone assumed that she was going to bed, and Jake took it as a cue to start gathering their things to prepare to leave for their hotel.

But Mrs. Vanderwaal returned to the living room, carrying a big gray metal box in one hand and two small framed photos in the other. She laid the box on the floor at Peter's feet. If she had planted a bomb, Peter could not have been more surprised.

"What is this, Mother?" he asked.

Mrs. Vanderwaal carefully placed the two small frames on top of the box. She aligned the larger of the two with the sides of the box. "They'll fit," she said, almost to herself.

"Well, dear," she began, "this is the box I gave you when you were in Epiphany for your father's funeral."

"I know what it is, Mother. I still have traces of black-and-blue from the crushing it gave my thighs as I ran to the plane."

"Have you looked in it?"

"A little. I found the tablet, Mother, but, honestly, I haven't had the time to look beyond that. I'll take care of it now."

"I was hoping you would take the time before the show, but you didn't."

"So am I being criticized for something else I didn't do—like not posting a No Bubble Gum Allowed sign?"

"Don't be so sensitive, dear. I simply didn't want you to worry when you notice that the box is gone."

"Where is the box going?"

"I'm taking it with me."

"Taking it with you? Where?"

"Well, dear, you know it was a dream of your father's and mine to travel the country in a Winnebago, but after he came down with his kidney problems and needed the dialysis three times a week, we couldn't do it. So before he took to the hospital that last time, he made me promise to buy a Winnebago."

"All right, Mother. When do you plan on doing this?"

"I already have, dear."

"What about the house?"

"I've sold the house, dear."

"You're leaving Epiphany?"

"Yes, dear, I am."

"You're going to travel by yourself."

"Yes, dear, I am."

"You surprise me."

"Well, you know what they say, dear. 'It's a wise child that knows his own mother.'"

"Mother! That's not it at all It's not what *they* say. It's

Shakespeare. And Shakespeare says, 'It is a wise father that knows his own child.'"

"Is that it, dear? He should have said it the other way around. 'It's a wise child that knows his own father.'"

Peter leaned over and tapped the metal box. "When you gave this to me, the word *Winnebago* did not even cross your lips."

"You had a lot on your mind, dear. Getting ready for this show."

"Exactly, Mother. And that is the very reason I did not have an opportunity to open that box again."

"And the show was the very reason I gave you the box."

"This show, Mother? My Once Forbidden show?"

"Yes, dear. *This* show."

"But what I saw was only part of a story Dad wrote."

"Yes, dear, but there's more. I had hoped that you'd look at all these papers before your show. I thought they might be useful to you."

"Mother, if you are trying to make me feel guilty, it's working."

"I know, dear."

Mrs. Vanderwaal picked up the two old black-and-white photos. "I'm taking these with me, too. They weren't in the box. I brought them with me. I don't think they'll be damaged by the trip. I do intend to drive with the windows open." Mrs. Vanderwaal handed Jake the first picture. "This is the one I kept on my desk when I worked for the city of Epiphany." Jake moved over on the sofa to make room for Mrs. Vanderwaal to sit between them. Peter sat on the arm. The photo showed three young people sitting on a tower. Amedeo recognized the tower as one of the three that stood high on a hill in Epiphany and that Jake took care of. In the picture the tower was still unfinished, not much taller than either of the girls. Peter was sitting on top of the tower, one of his hands on the head of each of the girls. All three were mugging for the camera.

Mrs. Vanderwaal pointed to one of the girls and said to Amedeo, "That's your mother."

"My mother?"

Peter said, "Your mother and I grew up in the same neighborhood in Epiphany."

Jake laughed. "What was it Mrs. Vanderwaal just said? 'It's a wise child that knows his own mother.'"

Amedeo said defensively, "I knew that. I definitely knew that Peter knew Mother before you did."

He returned the framed photo to Mrs. Vanderwaal, and she offered the other picture to them. "This is the other one I'm taking with me." The photo was so old that the whites were yellow and the blacks were umber. There were two young men standing on either side of a table. The men looked enough alike to be twins of different ages; they were holding up champagne glasses, as if to toast each other. There were candles on the table and a picture calendar on the wall above the table. Amedeo had seen the photo before. It used to sit on the mantel in the living room of Mrs. Vanderwaal's house in Epiphany.

Mrs. Vanderwaal pointed to the younger man on the right of the picture. "That is Peter's father," she said, "and the other young man is—*was*—his father's brother, Pieter. Peter is named for him. This was long ago. In Amsterdam." Mrs. Vanderwaal held the picture to her heart. "It will keep me company while I'm on my trip."

"Mother," Peter said, "I think you're being very theatrical."

"Am I, dear?"

"Yes, you are," Peter answered. "You know that being theatrical is my job."

"Well, dear, I'm sorry if I intruded."

Peter got up from his chair and threw his arms out. "Come here," he said. "Peter needs a hug." When Mrs.

Vanderwaal loosened herself from Peter's hug, he held her at arm's length and said, "You know, Mother, I do worry about you. I worry if you'll be safe, driving yourself all around the country in a Winnebago."

"Oh, Peter, dear. How nice of you to worry, but I have insurance—"

"That's good."

"—and I got one of those car phones. I'll give you the number. But we must keep all our calls brief. It's very expensive."

"Good."

"And I have a can of Mace."

"Mother! Mother, what good will that do you? Are you planning on baking cookies?"

"Mace, dear, is not always a spice. It's also pepper spray. For protection. I wouldn't leave home without it." Mrs. Vanderwaal smiled. "Have I upstaged you again, dear?" she asked.

"Like nobody ever has before," he said. "Any more surprises, Mother? When are you leaving?"

"Tonight."

"And that isn't a surprise?"

"I suppose it is, dear."

"Where is your car?"

"My Winnebago is parked down the street. I didn't

think the people in this apartment house would enjoy having an RV in their parking lot."

"The Winnebago is here? In Sheboygan?"

"Yes, dear. I drove it from Epiphany."

"Mother," he said, "do you know what Buckminster Fuller said about the caterpillar?"

"Is he another Shakespeare, dear?"

"There is only one Shakespeare, Mother."

"So will you tell me what Mr. Fuller said?"

"Buckminster Fuller said, 'There is nothing in a caterpillar that tells you it's going to be a butterfly.'"

"That's lovely, dear, but I've always known I had wings. Isn't there a stage between caterpillar and butterfly?"

Peter hugged her again. "Yes, Mother. It's called a chrysalis. The wings are there, invisible and under a hard protective cover."

Mrs. Vanderwaal leaned into her son's embrace before breaking away. She thumped the top of the metal box. "A hard protective cover. Yes, dear."

"Is there a butterfly in there?"

"A hero."

"With wings?"

"A hero, dear. Not an angel. You'll see."

15

THE LIBRARY IN MRS. ZENDER'S HOUSE WAS AN ENORMOUS room with what appeared to be a walk-in fireplace. Two walls had shelves from floor to ceiling. Every shelf was stacked with books and pictures in silver frames, small bronze figures, and glass objects (all of which needed cleaning). Mrs. Zender sat at the library table and pored over small items; Mrs. Wilcox had asked her to sort those she wanted to keep from those she wanted to sell.

Since William had given Amedeo his own china marking pencil, they shared chores, and when the day was over, they could not reliably tell who had done what.

They were polishing one of the several pairs of andirons that Mrs. Zender would not be taking with her—there would be no fireplaces in the Waldorf—when Mrs. Zender said, "Mr. Zender loved having a fire in the fireplace. When Daddy built this house, the only fireplace was in the living room. When Mr. Zender added the library and the master bedroom wing, he included a fireplace in each room and enlarged the dining room so that he could add a fireplace there as well. Mr. Zender had the architect draw up plans for a fireplace in the master bath, but for some engineering or scientific reason, it couldn't be done. Something to do with chimneys and exhaust fans. Who knows?

"We certainly had a plentiful supply of kindling and fire logs from Daddy's mill, but I can tell you Mr. Zender never could start a fire." She looked mischievously at Mrs. Wilcox, who blushed. "But he was no Boy Scout, either." Mrs. Wilcox blushed again.

"Oh, well," Mrs. Zender continued, "Mother always said that Mr. Zender had other talents. He was good-looking, and I think Mother put looking good right up there with the harpsichord, an instrument that has limited performance time and requires a great deal of maintenance." Then before putting her eyeglasses back on, Mrs. Zender stole a glance at Amedeo and William to make sure they were in on her joke. "Of course, Mr. Zender couldn't play the harpsichord, either."

There was so much stuff in the room that some things were on the steps of the ladder that rolled along the top of the shelves. Those had to be removed before Amedeo and William could begin to empty the shelves. Mrs.

Wilcox stood by, holding a yellow lined tablet and a pen, listing each item as it was taken down. From one of the ladder's steps, William took a framed menu from a French restaurant that had a squiggle of a drawing and a signature.

When he handed it to her, Mrs. Zender said, "Sandy Calder. That is, *Alexander Calder*, the artist who does those mobile things. He had dinner with Mr. Zender and me in Paris. He was a jolly man. He signed this menu instead of the check. I didn't mind, but Mr. Zender did." She laid the menu on the desk. "Don't bother to list this, Mrs. Wilcox. I'll take it with me."

On the highest shelf to the left of the giant fireplace was a row of books with foreign titles. William blew the dust off their tops and sent up a cloud that made him sneeze. Amedeo stood at the bottom of the ladder to take the books from him. "Don't drop those," Mrs. Zender said. "They are signed first editions."

"Oh?" Mrs. Wilcox said. "Used books are a specialty, Mrs. Zender."

"These books are not *used*, Mrs. Wilcox. I've never read them."

Amedeo read off the titles. *"L'Étranger, L'Être et Le Néant, Le Deuxième Sexe . . ."*

Mrs. Zender smiled. "Yes," she said. "Gifts from fans. All of them. They all wanted to sleep with me." Her smile broadened as she watched Mrs. Wilcox turn a shade of merlot, then she complimented Amedeo on his French. "Your accent is quite good. Where did you study?"

"New York," he answered. "I know that's not an excuse."

Mrs. Zender paused a minute before her laugh rumbled up. "Touché!" she said.

Mrs. Wilcox was returning to her natural color when Amedeo said, "*Le Deuxième sexe*, *The Second Sex*, was written by a woman. Simone de Beauvoir."

Mrs. Zender smiled. "Yes," she said. "Simone."

"And?"

"*And* read the inscription."

He opened the book to the title page and translated as he read, "'Dearest Aida, your Cherubino was superb! Simone.'"

"You see, bitch *or* boy, I was superb."

Amedeo examined the spine of the next book that William handed him. "*From Here to Eternity* by James Jones," he read. "This one is by an American."

"Yes," Mrs. Zender said. "James Jones. *Mon cher* Jimmy. He was living in a beautiful *maison* on the Ile St. Louis, in the heart of Paris, when he gave that to me. Jimmy's place was party central. He was the most generous man I've ever met. Of course, Hemingway hated him."

Amedeo asked, "Why did Hemingway hate him?"

"For the same reason Mailer did. They hated his success. He was not *literary* enough for them. I say, they shouldn't have come to his parties."

Mrs. Zender put on her thick black-rimmed glasses and started leafing through the book. "Of course, I've never read it, but I did see the movie. There was scene on the beach that caused quite a scandal at the time. I enjoyed that very much."

Mrs. Wilcox suggested, "These here books ought to be looked at by a proper expert, Mrs. Zender. I can call in a dealer I know."

Mrs. Zender looked up at Mrs. Wilcox, removed her glasses, and rested her elbow on the library table. She twisted her eyeglasses in slow circles with only the smallest movement of her wrist. Then, almost dreamily, she said, "I'll take these autographed first editions with me." She shook her head as if to bring herself back into focus, put her glasses back on, and sighed dramatically. "Putting my past on a shelf."

Mrs. Wilcox said cheerfully, "There's always a market for

matched sets of these here leather bounds, Mrs. Zender. Sometimes decorators, they buy leather-bound books by the lineal foot to fill up the shelves in them mansions they're building over on the west side."

"I live in a mansion, Mrs. Wilcox. Those places are not mansions. They are constructions that come in a kit with enhancements from a Chinese menu of features. They feature features."

Mrs. Wilcox smiled. "Yes, ma'am. But that's prob'ly where they'd be goin' unless I got ahold of a book dealer. You might could get more money for them from a regular used-book dealer."

"Most of them are in German." Mrs. Zender held one of the books at arm's length, turned it so that she could examine the spine. "German," she said, "was Mr. Zender's native tongue. He was Austrian, you know. Viennese, actually. A very proud people, the Viennese. They think they are above the other Austrians, and only God knows where the Austrians themselves think they are. I'm sure they can't find anyone important enough to discuss it with. A very masculine language, German." She laid *From Here to Eternity* on the table and said, "I haven't read a book in years. Every now and then I read a review in a magazine at the beauty parlor, and sometimes I think I would enjoy reading an entire book, but I allow the thought to pass." She surveyed the room. "They certainly do look handsome up there, don't they? We'll let the decorators have them, Mrs. Wilcox. Many are the McMansions that need shelves of red Moroccan-leather-bound books. There is no better way to ensure that they will remain unread."

William came down from the ladder and wheeled it to the next section of shelves. Amedeo was to take a turn up on the ladder and hand things down to William. He had climbed only to the middle rung when he saw a picture in the far back corner of a shelf.

The shelf was empty except for one book and the picture. The book was *To Kill a Mockingbird*. Amedeo had just read it in paperback as an assignment in Social Studies. Mrs. Zender's copy was hardback and still had its original dust jacket. Amedeo pulled it from the shelf and held it in his hand for a minute. There is something telling about a book that has been read, and even before he opened it, he knew that this copy had been. Amedeo couldn't resist looking at the title page. It was not inscribed, but it was autographed. He was impressed.

He said nothing as he handed it to William, who passed it on to Mrs. Zender. She glanced at it perfunctorily, and with a nod of her head, indicated that Mrs. Wilcox was to list it for sale. Mrs. Wilcox put a small numbered Post-it on it and made a note of its number on her preliminary list.

Amedeo turned back to the cubby to retrieve the only other object that was in this section of shelves. It was a framed drawing wedged in the corner. The frame was a little tall for the height of the space, and could not stand fully upright and so was both angled and catercornered in the back. Amedeo had to wrestle it loose. He did not want to scratch the shelf or shatter the glass by warping the frame, so he held his breath as he worked.

When it came free, he saw that unlike the elaborately framed paintings elsewhere in her house, this painting— a drawing, really—was held in a simple, well-made wooden frame of the sort that Jake approved. In the center there was a spot of cleared glass, a window like the one that had appeared on the top of the vintage waffle iron after he had wiped it with a wet paper towel. Amedeo picked off a shred of paper towel that was caught between the bevel of the frame and the glass. Through the porthole in the grime, he saw that he was holding a drawing of a nude. Probably pencil. Possibly pen. There was a bit of color. Red. The drawing itself was slightly larger than a sheet of paper from a school tablet.

Amedeo carried it down the ladder himself.

Mrs. Zender looked up. "What have you there?" she asked, reaching for it.

Amedeo did not hand it to her, and she did not insist. "I'll be careful," he said as he walked with it to the kitchen. William followed.

"What are you doing?" William asked.

"I think I found something," Amedeo answered.

"What?"

"I won't know until I clean it off."

"You better be careful."

"I said I would be."

"Don't run water on it."

"I know that. I just want to clean it enough to see."

"I think someone already tried."

"Yeah, I think so too."

Amedeo applied a little Windex to a paper towel and gingerly cleaned the glass. It was a drawing of a woman. Her face was in profile, and she was looking over her shoulder as if she were mooning the viewer. There was a wash of red paint that followed the curve of her hip. Amedeo examined it coolly.

"A naked lady," William said.

"A nude," Amedeo corrected. "Jake always tells me that there's a difference between naked and nude. Jake insists that even if they are men, they are to be called nudes. In art, for some reason, there are a lot more nude women than there are nude men, even though a single fig leaf doesn't cover as much on a female."

As he continued to clean the glass, Amedeo thought about what Mrs. Zender had said about the ninety percent and the ten percent, and he suddenly understood the difference between naked and nude. Naked shows the ten percent, but nude reveals the other ninety. Out loud he muttered, half to himself, "There is definitely a difference between naked and nude."

William said, "Tell me what it is—in a way that wouldn't make Ma blush."

Amedeo replied, "Naked *shows*, but nude *reveals*." Not that the rest of it—the part about the ninety percent and the ten percent—would have made Mrs. Wilcox blush, but for reasons not entirely clear to him Amedeo was not yet ready to share the conversation he had had with Mrs. Zender at the Dairy Queen.

The drawing deserved a better cleaning than he was giving it, but he couldn't let Windex and paper towels do one thing more. The rest of the cleaning would require softer, finer tools and far more time.

Amedeo carried the drawing over to Mrs. Zender. "Oh, this," she said, holding it at arm's length until she put her glasses on. "Come see this, Mrs. Wilcox." Mrs. Wilcox came forward. "This is *The Moon Lady*. That's what Mr. Zender called it when he gave it to me. It was a wedding gift." She extended the drawing and a magnifying glass to Amedeo. "Can you read the signature, Amedeo? It's there somewhere in the upper right, I think. Can you read what it says?"

Amedeo said, "I can read it without the magnifying glass, Mrs. Zender. It says 'Modigliani.'"

"Ah, yes," she replied. "Modigliani. He was Italian. Like my mother."

"I know him," Amedeo said. "We have the same first name."

"That is so," she said. "I forgot he had a first name. You do have that in common."

"And something else. He was Jewish."

"Is that so?" Mrs. Zender said. "Jewish."

"Are you named for him?" Mrs. Wilcox asked. "Being that your daddy is an artist and all."

"No. I was named for my grandfather."

"Was your grandfather a Jew?"

"One was. Not the Amedeo one. He was Amedeo Bevilaqua. I am a Kaplan by marriage."

"So what do you know about this Amedeo? Amedeo Modigliani?"

"I know some poems my father taught me."

"Tell us the poems, dear," Mrs. Wilcox urged.

"They're by a woman named Phyllis McGinley. My father said that all the kids in art history used to say them." Amedeo recited:

HOW TO TELL PORTRAITS FROM STILL-LIFES
Ladies whose necks are long and swanny
Are always signed Modigliani
But flowers explosive in a crock?
Braque.

ON THE FARTHER WALL, MARC CHAGALL
One eye without a head to wear it
Sits on the pathway, and chicken,
Pursued perhaps by astral ferret,
Flees, while the plot begins to thicken.
Two lovers kiss. Their hair is kelp.
Nor are the titles any help.

The Modern Palette
Picasso's Periodic hue
Is plain enough for any dullard.
The simple red succeeds the blue,
And now the Party-colored.

They applauded, and Amedeo took a little bow like the one he had seen Peter take after making his *welcome, everyone* remarks at the gala.

Mrs. Wilcox said, "Bein's it was a wedding gift, this little drawing must be very valuable to you, Mrs. Zender. I'm sure you'll be wantin' this for the Waldorf. For the shelf of your past."

"No," she said firmly. "I'm sure the work of a dead Jewish artist is worth a lot of money."

"If it's as valuable as all that, Mrs. Zender, don't you think you might could send it to Christie's or Sotheby's or one of them other famous auction houses? They'll know how to get the best price for it."

"No," Mrs. Zender said. "I don't want that."

Without raising an eyebrow, without doing a single thing that would betray her surprise, Mrs. Wilcox coded the drawing and put it on the list of things she would recommend to Bert and Ray.

Mrs. Zender picked up the copy of *To Kill a Mockingbird*

and said, "I changed my mind. I'm taking this to the Waldorf." Looking at Amedeo she said, "I once wrote to Harper Lee and told her that she ought to make an opera of her book."

"Did she answer?"

Mrs. Zender replied, "I don't know. I don't always open my mail."

16

THE TIME HAD COME.

It was late afternoon on the last Wednesday before the sale, and Bert and Ray were to be let in.

For the occasion, Mrs. Zender wore a silver lamé wide-legged pantsuit. She had affixed a long lavender scarf over one shoulder and drawn it across her chest and tied it at her waist. On the arm opposite the knot, she wore a noisy assortment of bangle bracelets that reached halfway to her elbow.

Immediately after the introductions, Mrs. Wilcox started her solicitations. She asked Ray, How was his cholesterol? Any new allergies? And Bert, How was his blood pressure? She invited them into the music room. It was in that room that she had gathered all the small, moveable items she thought would be of particular interest to them. Four of the Chippendale chairs had been carried there as examples and for them to sit in. As soon as Bert and Ray had wedged themselves into the chairs, Mrs. Wilcox offered them iced tea that she had flavored with mango. She had made a pitcher of plain iced tea as well, in case Ray was allergic to mango. Neither was allergic to mango, but Ray asked if she had sweetened it. He was watching his carbohydrates.

Bert and Ray were as coolly polite to Mrs. Zender as the telephone saleslady had been, but Amedeo noticed that their smiles, like hers, were an invitation to make Mrs. Zender a shared joke. But Mrs. Wilcox passed, just as Amedeo had.

Amedeo went with William to fetch the mango-flavored iced tea. He was feeling uneasy. Resentful. From the minute Bert and Ray said hello, Amedeo felt a chill come over the house. Everything suddenly looked shabby again.

As soon as he knew that no one but William could hear him, he said, "You would definitely think that Elvis has entered the building."

William smiled. "I warned you. Ma's attitude toward Bert and Ray is borderline religious. They are her holy couple, and don't expect it to let up. Just let me know if she starts in sayin' *thee* and *thou*."

Amedeo laughed.

When they returned with the iced tea, Mrs. Wilcox was saying, "You know, Bert and Ray, you are not limited to choosing only from among these here pieces. I just thought that these pieces were prime, and I wanted y'all to have first pick. There are other things throughout the house, but some of them were just too awkward to carry, so we can take a look around." They started their tour of the house. William went with them.

Amedeo stayed behind with Mrs. Zender.

As soon as they left, Mrs. Zender took in a deep breath, which she let out slowly through pursed lips. Right before his eyes, she grew as limp as a bouquet of Mylar balloons that had been sitting out for an hour too long. She handed Amedeo her glass of iced tea. "I'll have champagne," she said. "I've got a bottle chilling in the refrigerator." He started toward the kitchen. "No plastic," she said, "the stems always come off."

"I know. My godfather taught me that."

"Good for him. Remember it. No information about champagne is trivial."

"Where will I find the champagne flutes?" Amedeo asked.

"Somewhere in the inventory I'll be taking with me to the Waldorf."

As he walked to the kitchen, Amedeo realized that for

the first time there was no music in the hallway. The saddest music in the world could not be as sad as the silence in those dismantled rooms. But music was not the only thing that he sensed was coming to an end. Bert and Ray were intruding into a world that had become as close as the un-air-conditioned air they breathed.

When he returned with the champagne, Mrs. Zender's posture was less limp, but her majesty had not yet returned. He took a seat beside her. She sipped champagne. He sipped mango-flavored iced tea. He allowed his eyes to circle the room. Every item there was prime, chosen by Mrs. Wilcox and available to Bert and Ray for purchase. Each piece seemed to be the diary of a day's work. The sterling silver: the day he and William had a misunderstanding, followed by an understanding. The Meissen candlesticks: that day, he got his marking pencil. The Chippendale chairs: Mrs. Zender's mock dinner party. *The Moon Lady*: the library. But *The Moon Lady* was an unfinished entry.

Amedeo got up to look at the price tag: five thousand dollars.

William had taught him that pricing was tricky. Mrs. Wilcox had to be fair to both the seller and to the buyer. Pricing something too low may make it easy to sell, but may also be cheating the seller of a fair price. Pricing something too high may raise the seller's profit and the liquidator's commission, but can also make it too hard to sell. Dealers like Bert and Ray had to buy at a good price so that they could resell at a profit.

Five thousand dollars was the price Mrs. Zender herself had suggested.

Amedeo had heard enough adult conversations to know that most of them were about numbers: How big? How old? How long? But mostly they discussed: How much? In his mother's company, the numbers were usually about real estate, but he had heard enough conversations from Jake's friends to know that *how much* also counted in the art world, and he also knew that five thousand dollars was a lot of money but not nearly enough for an original drawing by a dead Modern artist, or as Mrs. Zender kept reminding him, a dead *Jewish* Modern artist.

Amedeo looked over at her, sitting there in her NASA moon-landing pantsuit. She sighed occasionally but said nothing. With each sip of champagne, though, her spirit inflated a little.

The tour group returned. They stood in the hall just outside the music room. William followed, carrying a folding luggage rack from one of the upstairs guest rooms. He put it down in the hall and wrapped a red SOLD sign around one of the legs. Mrs. Wilcox asked Bert and Ray if they were interested in the Bibendum chair that was in the upstairs sitting room.

Ray said, "You must mean Biedermeier."

Mrs. Wilcox was leaning over her clipboard to check her notes when Mrs. Zender's voice rang out. "No, gentlemen, she does not mean Biedermeier. She means Bibendum."

Bert said, "I can't remember what period Bibendum might be."

"It's not a period, Mr. Grover. Bibendum is the name of the Michelin Man. The chair was designed to look like a stack of Michelin tires, and like the tires themselves, the chair is French. Designed by Eileen Gray, who was Irish. If you must know a period, it is Art Deco."

Mrs. Wilcox said, "Yes. It's Art Deco. You might could take another look at it."

Ignoring Mrs. Zender, Bert addressed Mrs. Wilcox. "You know, Dora Ellen, Huntington Antiques does not do well with Modern art."

Mrs. Zender was not to be ignored. "Messrs. Grover and Porterfield," she called out, "you two are not the first people I've known to malign Modern art. There's a long history of people before you who have done it more vociferously and more effectively. I think it best, gentlemen, that

I withdraw the Bibendum chair. It is no longer for sale. I shall take it with me to the Waldorf."

Mrs. Wilcox said, "I'll just remove it from all the sales lists, Mrs. Zender."

Bert and Ray made an awkward entrance into the music room. They took a few minutes to survey the pieces there, and their focus almost immediately went to *The Moon Lady*, which had been placed in the center of an assortment on the lid of the closed baby grand. Bert reached for it and said, "What do you think, Ray? Do you think we'll be arrested for dealing in pornography if we display this in our shop?"

Ray replied, "If it's old enough and expensive enough, it's not pornographic, it's antique."

Mrs. Zender spoke up. "It is not antique. It is Modern art. And like the Bibendum chair, it too is French."

Without trying to hide his sarcasm, Ray pointed to the signature. "And is this Modigliani Irish?" Ray pronounced it "Moe-DIG-lee-ahn-nee."

Amedeo spoke up. "No," he said. "Italian. Modigliani was Italian." He took delight in pronouncing the painter's name "Moh-deelee-AH-nee" as he had been taught to do when he learned the poems. He knew that he was showing off and that Ray would be insulted.

Ray picked up on it. "How do you say it?"

"Say what?" Amedeo asked, stalling for time. What he was doing could not possibly be helping Mrs. Wilcox, but he seemed unable to help himself.

"The painter's name. How do *you* say it?"

Amedeo swallowed. "Moh-deelee-AH-nee. The *g* is silent."

"Is that French?"

"No," Mrs. Zender said emphatically. "As the young man just told you, the name is Italian. Modigliani"—she pronounced it with the silent *g*—"was Italian. What makes the drawing French is that Modigliani"—the silent *g* again—"drew it in France. French is what we commonly call things from France. Modigliani"—the silent *g*— "drew it in Paris, which happens to be in France. The capital city, actually."

Then Mrs. Zender stood up. "I am retiring to my room," she announced. She held her champagne glass at arm's length and swept it around the room, almost making a full circle. When she stopped suddenly, the fabric of her silver lamé pants wrapped around her legs like a swirl of soft frozen yogurt. She lifted her glass and—full tilt— drank the last few drops of champagne. She laid the empty glass on top of the piano, which Mrs. Wilcox had covered with a quilt. The glass teetered ever so slightly. Ray rescued it and held it awkwardly, like a stage prop. He pinched the stem between the thumb and forefinger of one hand and nervously rubbed the bottom with the other.

Mrs. Zender was now standing in the door with her arms extended outward at shoulder height. Her wingspan filled the archway from doorjamb to doorjamb. She waited until every eye was on her and Ray had stopped rubbing the bottom of the champagne flute. Slowly she swept one hand across her chest, followed it with the other, and columnlike, waited again. Then she lifted one hand—only one—and extended her arm. Like a Roman princess standing in the royal box, she announced, "Gentlemen, let the games begin." She bowed her head and swept out of the hall in an eddy of silver lamé.

Bert and Ray crumpled into the Chippendales. Without even looking at William, Ray handed the champagne glass to him. William carried it into the kitchen without being told to do so.

Amedeo followed.

"What happened just now?" Amedeo asked.

William said, "Happens all the time. People hate having their things looked at and judged. It's like an attack on their taste."

"Do you think that's all?"

"'Course not."

"What else?"

"I think Mrs. Zender doesn't like Bert and Ray."

"I can understand that. Definitely."

William laughed.

When William and Amedeo returned to the music room—they hadn't been gone long—the Meissen candlesticks had a red SOLD tag on them, and so did the antique brass fireplace tools. Ray was looking over Mrs. Wilcox's shoulder as she was checking items off her master list before writing them down on the sheet that would become his and Bert's bill of sale.

Bert had picked up *The Moon Lady* again. He said to his partner, "Your call, Ray."

There was no music in the room, but Amedeo's head was full of sound. He heard Mrs. Zender's exquisite nonchalance about how collectible Modigliani had become. He heard her saying, "He is the darling of art collectors now. He did something that art collectors love: He died young." But the question Amedeo could not stop asking himself was why Mrs. Zender was willing to sell *The Moon Lady* at all, let alone for five thousand dollars, and he knew—he knew in his heart that she didn't want to sell it to Bert and Ray.

Bert was still holding *The Moon Lady.* "Yes or no, Ray."

Amedeo spoke up. "It's a no."

"What did you say?"

"Mrs. Zender has withdrawn *The Moon Lady.*"

"Why didn't she tell us? She could have told us that instead of lecturing us about Paris being the capital of France. We know that Paris is the capital of France, don't we, Bert?"

Bert asked, "Why didn't she tell us herself?"

Amedeo had pitched his tent of lies, and now he had to live in it. "She told me." He looked to William for help.

William acknowledged him with a slight tilt to the angel on his shoulder and then said to Bert, "Mrs. Zender is used to having people."

Amedeo picked it up from there. "When you left for the tour, she said she decided to keep the drawing. She likes Modigliani"—he enjoyed not pronouncing the *g*—"too much . . . and you don't like Modern." Saying, "Excuse me," Amedeo took the drawing from Bert. He started to peel the price sticker from the glass.

Bert looked at Amedeo suspiciously. "Do you know about the Chinese screen?"

William answered for him. "Yes, sir, he does. I told him."

Ray said, "I just got to wondering if you and your little

friend are holding this back, the same way you did with that Chinese screen from the Birchfield estate."

William started to say, "We didn't hold back—"

But his mother interrupted. "I am right red-faced about all this. Please forgive me." Bert and Ray concentrated on Amedeo's removing the price label from the glass.

Turning to Amedeo, Mrs. Wilcox said, "Amedeo, dear, will you please to run *The Moon Lady* back up to Mrs. Zender with my apologies? Tell her I understand. Bert and Ray, I do hope you understand, too. I should have done more checking. I apologize again. But I'm hoping that little unpleasantness won't stop you from enjoying all these other nice things William and I picked out for you to look at. Like, can you take a look at this here Whiting's sterling silver? William, he polished every single piece, and I have researched all the hallmarks. It's the Lily pattern. You know Mrs. Zender's name was Aida Lily, and when she married, she received eighteen complete place settings. Everything. Including strawberry forks."

As he was leaving the room, Amedeo heard Bert say, "Nobody wants strawberry forks."

Mrs. Wilcox suggested, "You might could recommend that they do make nice cocktail forks."

Amedeo left the room holding on to *The Moon Lady*,

but instead of carrying it upstairs to Mrs. Zender's room, he left the house through the back door and took it to his room. When he returned to the Zender house, William was in the kitchen, wrapping the Meissen candlesticks in bubble wrap. William did not look up when he came in. Amedeo waited, then said, "I'm sorry about what happened."

"You embarrassed Ma."

"I know, and I am sorry."

"Mrs. Zender never did withdraw *The Moon Lady*, did she?"

"No, I did."

William finished wrapping the first candelabra before he looked at Amedeo. "You took *The Moon Lady* home with you, didn't you?"

"Yes."

"Would you call that stealing?"

"I don't think so. I don't expect to keep it, but I'm sure she didn't want Bert and Ray to buy it."

"Because?"

"I'm not sure. Mrs. Zender never said. I just know she doesn't want Bert and Ray to have it."

William immersed himself in one of his extended silences as he started wrapping the arms of the second candelabra. Amedeo nervously started cutting strips of bubble wrap and handing them to him. With both hands busy, taping the stem of the candlestick, William brushed his earlobe to the angel on his shoulder before he asked, "Did you ever tell Mrs. Zender about how you always wanted to discover something that no one knew had been lost?"

"Not directly. But she knows. Remember the day I told you? That was the day she kept coming into the kitchen, saying how hot it was and how she needed champagne to cool off. Like it was never hot and like she didn't always need champagne." Amedeo handed William another strip of bubble wrap.

William allowed his silence to continue until he finished wrapping one of the arms of the second candelabra. He examined his work, added another piece of tape, and then spoke. "I think *The Moon Lady* was a plant."

Amedeo said, "I didn't want to say so, but honestly, William, the thought crossed my mind, too."

William at last looked at him. "When?"

"When I saw it sitting by itself on a shelf, calling attention to itself with a book that every schoolkid can recognize. And partly cleaned like nothing else was."

"There's something else."

171

"What?"

William started a long silence. He was cutting a pad of bubble wrap for the bottom of the candelabra, and Amedeo waited. "Ma and I were all geared up to start work on the library that weekend you went up to Sheboygan. Mrs. Zender didn't decide she needed the weekend off—never said a word about it—until you told her that you were going to see an exhibit called Once Forbidden. She wanted you to be here when we started the library." Despite himself, Amedeo broke out a huge grin, which William did not return. "What I can't figure is, if she didn't want Bert and Ray to have it, why did she let it go that far?"

"She's spoiled. She wanted me to do it for her. Just like the day we went to Dig-It-All. She wanted the phones, but she didn't want to pick them out, so I did it for her. And then when we went to check out, she embarrassed me in front of the lady at the cash register."

"Like you embarrassed Ma in front of Bert and Ray. Ma don't deserve that."

"I know she doesn't, and I am sorry."

William picked up one of the candlesticks, and Amedeo started to pick up the other. William said, "I don't think you better go back in there. I don't think Ma or Bert and Ray need to see you again. Not tonight, anyway."

Amedeo said, "Please tell your mother I'm sorry."

"I ain't your people, Deo. You got to tell her that your-self." He pushed through the swinging door of the kitchen and was gone.

17

AMEDEO WAS EXHAUSTED. LIES, STEALING, AND BERT AND Ray had worn him out. Worst of all, though, was having William mad at him.

When he had snuck back into Mrs. Zender's house, he had hoped to find William alone—which he did—and find him rather amused at the whole incident. It was clear to Amedeo that William did not favor Bert and Ray the way that Mrs. Wilcox did. He had a faint hope that William would even be pleased with him for having pulled the sale of *The Moon Lady* out from under them. It took only one look at William's cold concentration on wrapping the candelabra for Amedeo to know that, polite and restrained as he had been in front of Bert and Ray, William was furious with him. And he had every right to be. Amedeo's lie had put both William and his mother in a bad place. He had challenged William's loyalty to him as a friend and a coworker, but worst of all, his lie had been a challenge to Mrs. Wilcox's integrity. In front of Bert and Ray, William had stayed cool and courteous, almost courtly. But Amedeo had embarrassed Mrs. Wilcox— embarrassed her terribly—yet despite her concern for the feelings of Bert and Ray, she, too, had closed ranks around him.

He owed Mrs. Wilcox a big apology. Definitely. It would take more than an apology, however big, to make it up to her.

He thought again about William's silence when he returned to Mrs. Zender's. It was angry. Infrasonic. Beyond William's worst. And he deserved it.

Why? he asked himself. Why had he risked William's friendship and Mrs. Wilcox's? What was there about Bert and Ray that had made him lie and steal?

He could deal with the stealing, because he still wasn't sure if what he did was really stealing if he meant to return it. And there was the possibility that it had been a plant, after all. There was the possibility that he was meant to find it. Even William thought so.

It was the lying that had hurt the most, and to be honest with himself, it wasn't Bert and Ray who made him do it. It was Mrs. Zender. He had lied for her, for the sake of something he thought she might want him to do. He had become her people.

But then he listened to himself, and he knew that if he lifted the quilt of lies inside his head, that if he told the truth out loud, he had to admit that he lied and stole not for Mrs. Zender and not because of Bert and Ray. He had done it for himself. For the part of himself that did not want to lose his chance to escape anonymity and discover something, the part of himself that wanted recognition.

Maybe another truth, the truth about *The Moon Lady*, would help him make up for the lies. He had to start asking some hard questions: Why was Mrs. Zender willing to sell *The Moon Lady* in the first place? Why would she hold on to a little drawing on a menu by Alexander Calder— *Sandy*—and sell a signed Modigliani that Mr. Zender had given her as a wedding gift? And if she didn't want it to sell, why had she priced it so low?

He could start by asking Mrs. Zender some of the same questions he had just asked himself, but he knew he wouldn't. Mrs. Zender didn't operate that way. Her secrets were in the large hidden self that she kept offstage.

If she had planted *The Moon Lady* for him to find—and he was more convinced than ever that she had—maybe what she really wanted was for him to find out the truth about it. The boys who discovered the cave of Lascaux had to call in the archeologists who had carbon dating to let the world know what they had discovered, and even the French soldier who found the Rosetta stone and immediately knew it was important, didn't know why. It took twenty-three years and a college professor to decode the writings to find out that it was the key to understanding hieroglyphics. Maybe that was the kind of discovery he was supposed to make about *The Moon Lady*: decoding and deciphering.

He would start now.

He set the drawing on the desk opposite his bed and lay down with his hands under his head and looked at it. And looked and looked. Forty-five seconds would be just a tap on the time he would spend looking at it.

It was already hauntingly familiar. Not because he had seen it at Mrs. Zender's. It was familiar to him in another way. There was recency, but there was also frequency. Amedeo knew that he had seen it before and seen it often. Inside his head Amedeo kept reviewing how Mrs. Zender reminded him of how Modigliani did collectors a favor by dying young and thereby becoming a dead *Jewish* Modern artist.

Amedeo took down his copy of the *Once Forbidden* catalog and looked for Amedeo Modigliani. All the artists were Modern. All were dead. Only one was Jewish. And it wasn't Modigliani. It was:

Marc Chagall: Degenerate because he was Jewish. The Jews—just by virtue of being Jews—by even a fraction of their heritage were the absolute worst contaminators of the Aryan race. What would happen to German culture if it allowed itself to be contaminated by Jews?

He again checked every picture in the catalog. Modigliani was not there.

He reread the introduction. The Nazis forbade artists to depict the male form as anything other than "heroic" and the female as anything other than "maternal" or "feminine." Surely, the Nazis would consider *The Moon Lady* doubly degenerate. Her neck was long and swanny (at least the part he could see was). And the artist who painted it was a Jew.

He reread *Once Forbidden* from cover to cover and recited the poem to himself. Braque, Chagall, and Picasso were all in the catalog, but Modigliani was not.

But Modigliani was somehow connected to Once Forbidden. He reviewed the evening of the *molto, molto magnifico* gala. There was champagne and Peter's welcoming remarks. There was the couple who spent all that time in front of the Braque and there was the boy with the pink bubble gum in front of the *Blue* Picasso.

There was something else about the *molto, molto* evening. Something significant. He remembered more:

Mrs. Vanderwaal's surprise at the after-party party in Peter's apartment. The Winnebago. The gray box she was taking with her. The two pictures she had shown them before putting them in the gray box.

One was the old, yellowed, black-and-white picture that showed Peter's father and his uncle, named Pieter, holding champagne glasses and toasting each other the way Mrs. Zender had toasted her audience in the music room. He had seen that picture before when they had visited Mrs. Vanderwaal in Epiphany.

Frequency and recency.

Amedeo jumped up from bed and checked his watch. It was after ten. But Sheboygan was on Central time. It would be an hour earlier there. He called his godfather.

"Do you have a problem, my son?" Peter asked in his Marlon Brando/Godfather voice.

Taking his cue from Peter, Amedeo answered, "Yes, Godfather, I have need."

"You may tell me, my son."

Amedeo told him the history of his work at Mrs. Zender's.

"What is her collection like?" Peter asked.

"Mostly peasant scenes in large, elaborate gold frames.

Mrs. Wilcox isn't even sending them to an art dealer. They're the sort that decorators want—along with the three feet of red books—which Mrs. Zender also has, by the way. Mrs. Zender is more interested in good music than in good art. She has a menu that Alexander Calder signed instead of signing the check. She's keeping that. She's keeping only one or two of the others for her new home."

Peter listened carefully and then said, "I don't understand. What is the problem, my son?"

"I think Mrs. Zender has a piece of Degenerate art. By Modigliani. Wasn't his work confiscated by the Nazis?"

"There was one Modigliani confiscated by the Goebbels Committee in 1937. An oil painting, *Portrait of a Woman*, or as they say, *Damenbildnis*. It was sold at auction. The *Damenbildnis* has a well-documented provenance; that is, it has proof of authenticity and past ownership. Everything sold at auction these days must have that. The *Damenbildnis* last changed hands in 1984. It is in a private collection, which, I'm sorry to tell you, is not Mrs. Zender's."

"Mrs. Zender's is a drawing, not a painting."

"Describe it to me, Deo."

"Pencil or crayon on paper, slightly larger than a sheet of tablet paper, buttocks facing out, face over her right shoulder, impish smile, no teeth showing, red wash of gouache or watercolor, brushstrokes clearly visible, no color on the body even though looking at it, you think pink."

"Well done, Deo. But I must ask, is her neck long and swanny?"

"You can't see too much of her neck," Amedeo answered seriously. Then he laughed. "Dad taught me that poem, but I almost forgot to tell you the most important thing: *Modigliani* is written in script in the upper right."

"Well, my son," he said, "I'm going to tell you the most important thing too. And because I am telling it, my important is more important than your important. Modigliani is very popular these days. People in art circles say that there were more works by Modigliani after he died than there were while he was living. His work is repro-duced on everything from T-shirts to coffee mugs to—"

"—calendars! That's it. I've seen it on a calendar, Peter."

"I'm not surprised. It is not called calendar art for nothing."

"Peter, do you remember the night of the gala opening of Once Forbidden?"

"Remember? Me, remember? Of course I remember. Was it or was it not a *magnifico* night to remember?"

"Do you remember the picture your mother showed us that night?"

"She showed us two. The one with your mother and—"

"The one with your dad as a young man. That's the one I need to see."

"You have already seen it."

"I need to see it again."

"Mother has it. It's keeping her company, remember? She showed it to all of us the night she disappeared in a cloud of Winnebago exhaust."

"Peter, please. I definitely need to see it."

"But you've seen it hundreds of times. Every time you came over to our house. It was always on the mantel in the living room. Don't you remember?"

"I remember. I know I've seen it *frequently*. But, Peter, please, I need to see it again."

"Why?"

"On the wall between your uncle Pieter and your father, there was a calendar."

"A 1942 calendar. Uncle had circled the date, September 4. They apparently were celebrating something."

"Peter, please, I need to see that calendar."

"Have you become one of those idiot savants who can figure out what day of the week September 4, 1942, was?"

"I don't mean to be disrespectful, Godfather, but they don't call them idiot savants anymore."

"What then?"

"They're autistic calendar savants. But I'm definitely not one of them. I want to see the picture on that calendar. I think it was by Modigliani."

"Modigliani was a Jew, remember? You don't for one minute think that a human female tushie painted by a Jew would be on a calendar in Amsterdam in the year 1942, do you?" Then, as if to answer his own question, he said, "Oh, my God. Mother was telling me something, wasn't she?"

"I think so."

"And the hero in the gray box—" Peter said, half to himself.

"Where is the box, Peter? Mrs. Zender's sale starts next weekend, and—"

"It's in a Winnebago. The only address I could possibly have for it is some double-digit interstate highway."

"May I call your mother? Please? She said she has one of those car phones."

"That phone costs a gazillion dollars a minute whether she's making a call or receiving one. That damn phone ought to be listed as a dependent. It costs more than my college tuition did."

"Can I call her? Please? I'll be brief, Peter. I promise. Please give me her number."

"I don't like having her talking on the phone while

she's driving. Mother's secret demon comes out when she's behind the wheel of any vehicle that has wheels and a motor. If she hears the urgency in your voice, she'll arrive with a police escort. And then won't you and your Mrs. Wilcox be embarrassed?"

Amedeo waited and said nothing. He knew what was coming.

It came.

Peter put on his Godfather voice again. "I'll make the call."

"Thank you, Godfather."

"You will need to look at some papers in that gray box."

"I will, Godfather. Thank you. I will."

"And you will need to kiss my ring."

"I will, Godfather, I definitely will."

"How often?"

"Many times."

18

For the first time in all the weeks they had been working together, Amedeo didn't wait until the bus was out of sight to meet up with William. He planted himself at the bottom of the bus steps, and as soon as William hit the sidewalk, Amedeo said, "I am mortified by the way I embarrassed your mother last night, and I want a chance to apologize."

As he expected, William did not answer immediately. They were walking side by side, Amedeo anxiously keeping up with William's long-legged pace. They were halfway to Mrs. Zender's when William suddenly stopped. Lost to worry, Amedeo had gone on for several steps before he realized that William was no longer at his side.

To his surprise William said, "Ma has been right wary of *The Moon Lady* ever since the day we found it."

Amedeo said hopefully, "Then she forgives me?"

"More than I do, and probably more than she should."

"I'd like to see her and explain."

"Ma suspects you know something about *The Moon Lady*. She's already guessed that you have something to tell."

"She's right. I think I do have something. I called my godfather last night."

And there on the street, out of sight and hearing range of Mrs. Zender's house, Amedeo told William about the old photograph from Amsterdam in the year 1942.

"So Mrs. Zender is being wily," William said. And then he smiled.

Amedeo watched his smile widen into the kind that he and William often shared when Mrs. Zender held out her champagne flute, and one or the other of them would wordlessly fill it.

There was a lot besides smiles that Amedeo and William shared at Mrs. Zender's. There was also her house, which was always a carnival of sights and sounds. Whenever they opened the door, they never knew if they would meet the lady or the tiger, for Aida Lily Tull Zender could be fierce and demanding or smiling and funny. She was always full of herself, but she was also always full of fun. She dressed up every day as if she were giving a performance, and yet she did not seem vain. Despite her theatricality, there was something genuine about her. She ordered everyone around as if she were royalty, yet she was not unkind. Despite her bossiness, there was something generous about her. She was full of commands, contradictions, and inconsistencies, but she was always interesting, and she touched both of them in ways they didn't have to admit or discuss. Being her friend was difficult but exceptional. Being her friend was a bond between them like a pledge to a fraternity.

William's smile had not faded before Amedeo said, "Mrs. Zender may be as wily as your mother is deep."

William accepted the compliment with quiet dignity.

Mrs. Vanderwaal's Winnebago was waiting in Amedeo's driveway. As soon as they saw it, they broke into a run. Amedeo knocked.

Mrs. Vanderwaal opened the door and said, "Yes, dear."

Amedeo introduced William, and Mrs. Vanderwaal said, "This is a lovely place you have here, Deo."

"Thank you," Amedeo replied. "Won't you please come in?"

As she stepped down from the Winnebago, she said, "Peter tells me that we have urgent business."

"Yes, we do. Definitely," Amedeo replied.

"Is William interested as well?"

Amedeo said, "William is primary."

"If that is so, Deo, dear, we'll need the gray lockbox. Would you please bring it? It's under my bed."

The French captain prying the Rosetta stone from the wall of the ancient desert fort was hardly as careful as Amedeo Kaplan sliding the gray metal box out from under Mrs. Vanderwaal's bed.

After eating a snack and having Amedeo explain why William was a principal in the matter, Mrs. Vanderwaal unlocked the box and took out all the papers that were on top. From under the loosely fitted metal panel on the bottom, she took a pad of yellow lined paper.

"I would like you and William to read this."

The paper was old—almost damp with age—and the edges were fuzzy and worn. The first page said:

THE STORY OF A LIFE, MINE
Written from Memory
by John Vanderwaal

They read the pages and came to:

The next bad year was 1942. Here comes now the story of how came I to America, and I became from

Johannes to John and from the three words van der
Waal, *I became one word* Vanderwaal, *like* van der
Bilt *became* Vanderbilt *and* Van Rosenfelt *became*
Roosevelt. *But never so rich or famous.*

The writing stopped in the middle of the page.

As Peter had done before him, Amedeo flipped through
the rest of the pages and found nothing. No mention of
The Moon Lady. No mention of Modigliani.

Mrs. Vanderwaal said, "There is more, dear." She
reached back into the gray box. "The rest of young
Johann's story is written on the back sheets of medical
forms. I'm sure you realized that the young Johann
who wrote all this was my husband, John. For the last ten
years of his life, John had to have dialysis three times a
week, so some days he would write on the backs of the
medical forms he had to sign." She waved a sheaf of thin
pink sheets, which were clipped together. "I tried to put
them in order by using the dates on the medical forms,
but dear John did not write chronologically. There are
repetitions and cross outs, but I think you boys will work
it out. Read it, Deo."

"Out loud?"

"Yes, dear. I want you to meet my hero."

He read.

*It is in April of this bad year that Jews were made to wear
the Yellow Star. Jews were not allowed to enter museums or
movie theaters. They were not allowed to work, and so many
Jews were selling off their beautiful things to get money to
live. The Germans had a lot of money, and they were greedy.
They wanted for themselves art and antiques and rugs, all
the things to show that they were "cultured" persons.*

Business at Pieter's shop was good.

*Late on one afternoon in September of 1942 a Nazi
officer came into Pieter's shop. Klaus and I were the only
ones in the gallery that day. The officer walked around the
shop. He walked slowly, but his eyes danced around the
room, lighting every now and then on a particular piece,
but never lingering on any one thing long enough to
betray a curiosity. He said little, but I could tell by his
accent that he was Austrian. He touched nothing. Before
heading toward the door, the officer asked Klaus if he was
the owner of the shop. Klaus said that he was not. The
officer pointed to me.*

—And this young man?

*—He is the brother of the owner. He helps with the
dusting and polishing.*

The officer took a few more steps around the gallery.

—I'm finding some of your pieces very interesting. I'm

finding that I should like to investigate some of these
pieces further.

—We should be most grateful, said Klaus.

—Very well, then. Tomorrow. I shall return tomorrow.

He walked toward the door with his hands behind his
back in that strange posture that I have come to know
from Nazi officers and the duke of Edinburgh. He
paused and said:

—Tomorrow I will speak with the owner of the shop.

His gloved hand came from behind his back, and he
started to reach for the door, but Klaus hurried over to
open it for him. So the Nazi stopped and instead raised
his hand to his face and brought his forefinger to his
lips. He tucked under his chin his thumb, and with his
forefinger, which was still in the glove, he rubbed his lips
up and down. Up, down.

—I advise you not to sell any interesting items
between now and then.

He tapped his finger to his lips twice and then asked me:

—How old?

—Fifteen years.

The officer's smile was ice. He repeated, "Tomorrow,"
and then he stepped outside from our shop.

Klaus collapsed in a chair.

—*At least he didn't say "Heil Hitler," said I, Johannes.*

—*Yes, he did. Oh, yes, he did, said Klaus.*

The following day, when I returned from school, I had a habit to look through the shop window, which I did. I saw then that the officer had returned. Two others were with him. They were of a lesser rank. Before I had a chance to reach the door to our shop, I caught the eye of my brother. With a small nod of his head, my brother, Pieter, motioned that I should look to the sign in the shop window: Closed.

So very quietly, I went around and entered to our shop from the back. I pressed my ear against the wall that was common to the back room and to the gallery.

I listened.

I heard them walking around, but the only voices I could hear were my brother and the Nazi officer, the Austrian. The voices were muffled, but I have had by then years of learning how to listen.

I heard the Nazi say "Verboten," which means "forbidden." I heard him say it at least once more. I heard more footsteps. All three of them were walking around. Then I heard "Alles Entartete." . . . More walking, and then destroy. *Then more footsteps and then* in the morning.

Then three voices said, "Heil Hitler."

This was loud and clear.

I waited now until I heard the door close before coming out from the back room. My brother, Pieter, was closing the shutters on the windows of the shop.

—Closed. Our gallery is closed, Johannes.

He grinned, but was not grinning.

—The Germans are taking over our shop.

—Are we Jewish?

—No.

—I heard the Nazi say forbidden. *He said that word. Have you done some business with a Jew?*

—Of course I have. Everybody has. The beautiful merchandise came from somewhere, you know.

—What is degenerate? *I heard also that word, Pieter.*

—Enough questions for now, Johannes. The shop is closed, and I am having a retirement party. Go now to our rooms and clean up. Then come back down to the gallery. Some of your questions will be answered.

I went upstairs. I splashed some water onto my face, and I smiled to myself, because when now I used the towel to dry my face, the towel caught in the stubble of my chin. I was thinking: I did not shave this morning. I was thinking: Soon I will need to shave every morning. I dropped the towel and looked again in the mirror. What was I thinking? Something terrible is happening, and I am thinking now about my chin hairs. I closed my eyes

e. l. konigsburg

and rubbed them until they hurt. I began now to tremble, and I braced myself on the bowl of the sink. I caught my face in the mirror, and I said to the face, "It has come. It has come." Louder, I said, "It has come." As I was leaving then the bathroom, I caught again my face in the mirror, and I whispered to the face, "Now it has come."

I went downstairs. Gerard, Jacob, and Klaus were lined up in the narrow hallway that led from the back room to the gallery. Each had his hands behind his back in imitation of the Nazi officer. I smiled when first I saw them. I started to walk down the narrow hallway. "A receiving line?" I asked. They did not answer but clicked their heels in unison. And now I noticed: Jacob, who was standing in the middle, was wearing on his lapel a yellow six-pointed Star of David. I asked:

—Are you a Jew?

—Yes.

Jacob tilted his head to the right where Klaus was standing. My eyes now fell on Klaus's lapel. Klaus had pinned on his lapel a bright Pink Triangle, the Rosa Winkel.

I knew already what the Pink Triangle meant, but I could not stop myself from asking.

—Are you a homosexual?

—Yes.

I heard then Jacob laugh.

—I, too, am a homosexual. The Nazis couldn't decide on yellow or pink for me, but they decided that being a Jew is worse.

Klaus and Gerard then laughed, too, but I could not join in.

They now nudged me down the hall in the direction of the gallery. My brother, Pieter, had quietly opened the door and was standing there within its frame.

Pieter, too, was wearing the Rosa Winkel.

The pages that followed were blank, and Amedeo, who sensed he was on the verge of tears, was grateful that he had to stop. William was enveloped in one of his silences; only his clenched jaw and reddened nostrils betrayed him.

Mrs. Vanderwaal said, "There's more to the story, dear. I have it here. Do you want me to read it?"

Both Amedeo and William nodded, and Mrs. Vanderwaal read.

The evening of the "retirement" party, we had many hugs and kisses, and then each of the friends brought out something that they had scrounged or saved. There was

bread and herring, and Gerard brought out some
chocolates.

Pieter asked Gerard to take a picture of him and me.
We stood on either side of a table that Pieter had moved
to the calendar wall. Pieter made a circle around the date
on the calendar: September 4, 1942. We two brothers
lifted our glasses in a toast to each other.

Amedeo interrupted. "That's the picture I asked for, isn't
it, Mrs. Vanderwaal?"

"Yes, dear, it is."

"Did you bring it?"

"Yes, I told you I did."

"May I see it now?"

"Not yet. I recommend that we read some more."

The following day Pieter insisted that I go to school
as usual. He said that it was important to act normal.

—I don't want you here when that Nazi officer
returns.

—But he knows I exist. He asked Klaus who I was.

—Yes, but he does not know that you live here, with
Klaus and me. You understand what I'm telling you,
Johannes? The Nazi thinks you live with a mother and a
father.

When I returned from school the following day, I found Gerard waiting. He was outside our building. He told me that Pieter was taken.

I knew what taken *meant. After a* razzia, *Jews were taken. Taken away to concentration camps. But I could not translate. Pieter had said already that we were not Jews.*

—*Taken? Where?*

—*Neuengamme. Klaus, too.*

I knew Neuengamme. Neuengamme was a labor camp in Germany where prisoners were worked to death, making bricks from mud they had to dig up with their bare hands. And they were made to carry bricks, still hot from the ovens with their bare hands.

—*And Jacob?*

—*To Auschwitz.*

—*And you, Gerard? Are you a* Rosa Winkel?

—*Yes, but I don't have yet the Pink Triangle. I am useful still. I am photographing the works of art in the Rijksmuseum. The Nazis love having records more than they hate homosexuals, and the Nazis don't make razzias of homosexuals as they do the Jews and the Gypsies. Homosexuals are less of a problem because we do not reproduce.*

—*Why then did they take Pieter and Klaus?*

—Because Pieter made a bargain. The officer came back this morning. Alone. And Pieter sold him a few items.

—What items?

—A few porcelains and a couple of pieces of art.

—Which art?

—The Degenerate. The Nazi told Pieter that for a price he would relieve him of certain forbidden works of art he had in his shop.

—What price?

For an answer Gerard handed to me two sheets of paper. One paper was a shop receipt. The other piece of paper was an official document, an Unbedenklichkeitserklärung, *what the Nazis called a* statement of harmlessness, *which in Nazi language was an exit visa.*

Gerard now put his forefinger under my chin for the purpose of lifting my eyes to see him. Gerard smiled sadly.

—If Pieter had been a Jew, there could not have been such a payment.

Mrs. Vanderwaal stopped reading. In a voice near to breaking, Mrs. Vanderwaal said, "My son, Peter, is named for his dear dead uncle."

Amedeo saw that Mrs. Vanderwaal's hands were trembling. He reached across the table and took the pages from her, and then he took her hands in his. His voice barely above a whisper, he said, "I think we're ready to see the picture, Mrs. Vanderwaal."

"There's more to the story, dear."

"I can see," Amedeo said, "but I think it can wait."

William solemnly nodded yes in agreement.

Mrs. Vanderwaal carefully evened the margins of the pages she had read and then laid them off to one side. Then she reached into the gray box and took out a heavy manila envelope. She pulled the photo from it and placed it on the table between Amedeo and William. Amedeo was grateful that it had a protective glass, for he feared his breath was so heavy it would dissolve film. He gasped. "That's *The Moon Lady* on the calendar, isn't it?"

"I can make out the signature," William said. "I can make out the capital *M* and the letters *o*, *d*, and *i*"—and smiling at Amedeo, he added, "And the silent *g*."

Mrs. Vanderwaal reached into her purse and took out a small magnifying glass. Amedeo used it to focus. "Look, look!" he called. "That drawing doesn't belong to the calendar. It is tacked above the dates. This photo is a message, isn't it, Mrs. Vanderwaal?"

She nodded yes. "This was something I had wanted my son, Peter, to investigate when he was preparing for Once Forbidden. After all, Modigliani was a Jew and his work was considered degenerate. No Dutch calendar would dare display the art of a Jewish artist, during the Nazi Occupation. Pieter asked to have this picture taken not only for sentimental reasons, but also for evidence." She reached again into the gray box. This time she took out a folder. Her hand was shaking again, so Amedeo opened the folder for her. One piece of paper was obviously an official form, full of stamps and signatures, and the other appeared to be an old-fashioned sales slip.

"Were these papers in the lockbox?"

"Yes, dear. Look at them. They answer some questions."

Amedeo said, "I can't read German."

Mrs. Vanderwaal said, "They're all in German, dear."

Amedeo replied, "A definite inconvenience."

William couldn't contain his impatience. "Deo! Take it down a couple degrees."

Mrs. Vanderwaal occupied herself by cleaning the lens of her magnifier. Then she pointed to the smaller of the two papers. "This is a receipt for 'one pair of candelabra, one small drawing in black crayon on paper, and a study— crayon on paper—of a female, by Klimt.' The name of the artist is deliberately scribbled."

In hopes of recovering some of his lost status but not to show off—definitely not to show off—Amedeo explained, "That would be Gustav Klimt, the Austrian artist who painted *The Kiss*?"

"Yes, dear, but he was also out of favor with the Nazis. His work was too sensual."

William gave Amedeo a slant-eyed look and turned to Mrs. Vanderwaal.

"Definitely too sensual," Amedeo added. "You also believe that the small drawing, the one in black crayon on paper, is Mrs. Zender's *The Moon Lady*, don't you?"

"I'm certain it is."

Pointing to the photograph, William said, "The date that is circled on the calendar in the photo is the same as the date on the sales receipt."

"Yes, dear."

Now it was Amedeo who was getting annoyed. William was taking over, and this was his Rosetta stone. Amedeo pulled the sales receipt closer and, working to get the small magnifier in focus, he studied the scribble at the bottom. He turned the paper upside down and every which way. He made out a letter—*Z!*—a capital *Z*, and the letters *e* and *n*. His heart skipped a beat. "That says Zender," he said, pointing to the scribble. "It must be Zender. That's my next-door neighbor. Mrs. Zender said that Mr. Zender gave *The Moon Lady* to her for a wedding present." At last, everything was fitting into place. "Mr. Zender must have been the Nazi officer who blackmailed Pieter. Mr. Zender was an Austrian and so was the Nazi officer. We have him, Mrs. Vanderwaal! We just have to—"

Mrs. Vanderwaal smiled. She tugged at the corner of the paper and gently slid it back across the table. She looked at it for a long time before shaking her head. "I've studied that word for more than fifty years, and my dear John did too. But, Deo, as I'm looking at it again, trying so hard to assign it to Zender, I just can't. I wish I could. But it says 'Zahlend,' which in German means 'Complete' or 'Paid.'"

Entropy! Total entropy! Everything was falling apart. He was not a boy falling into a cave and finding drawings on the walls. He was also not a cryptologist making sense of something someone else had discovered. He was no hero. He was still Amedeo Kaplan, the anonymous.

In a subconscious effort to hold himself together, Amedeo crossed his arms and hugged his shoulders. He leaned forward, not allowing himself to touch the picture or hardly to breathe on it. His focus fell on the candlesticks. Letting his arms go to pull the photo forward, he asked, "What about those candlesticks, William?" He pushed the picture toward his friend. "Don't they look like the Meissen ones that Bert and Ray bought?"

William examined the photo carefully. "Mrs. Zender's candelabra were double-branched. These are triple."

Mrs. Vanderwaal remained quiet as Amedeo noisily swallowed his disappointment. Then she slid the other slip of paper forward. "Why don't you look at this, Deo? It's the paper that gave John safe passage out of Holland. It's an exit visa, what the Nazis called a *Unbedenklichkeitserklärung*. This one has a signature and many stamps. The Germans love to stamp things. There are two stamps on the exit visa—one red and one black. The black square one has space for the date and place, and some of the stamp has obscured the writing. But you can read the place, Amsterdam, and the date, 04 September 1942. Those are consistent with the calendar and with the bill of sale. The red stamp is round, and it is not too difficult to read the signature."

"Does it begin with a *Z*?" Amedeo asked hopefully. Mrs. Vanderwaal didn't answer but allowed Amedeo to study the signature. "It's an initial *K* followed by a capital *E*—"

"Yes, dear. The Germans love capital letters."

"E-i-s-e-n-h-u-t-h. That would be Karl Eisenhuth."

"Karl Eisenhuth. You know him?"

"He's the acoustician who installed Mrs. Zender's sound system."

"Do you think he gave her the Modigliani?"

After first checking with Amedeo as if waiting for permission to answer, William said, "No. Mr. Zender gave it to her."

Amedeo shook his head. "It definitely was from Mr. Zender."

William nodded in agreement. "She said it was a wedding gift. They got married sometime in the 1950s."

"Where is Mr. Zender now?"

"As dead as Mr. Eisenhuth."

"And Mrs. Zender?"

"She's next door."

19

MRS. WILCOX WAS IN THE KITCHEN WORKING ON HER LISTS. Dealers and decorators were already calling. Apparently Bert and Ray also liked to be discoverers, so they had let a few of their colleagues know that they had gotten in first, and Mrs. Wilcox was checking their inquiries against her inventory.

Mrs. Zender was in full regalia, telling Mrs. Wilcox about a performance of Richard Strauss's *Salome* in which she had sung the role of Salome. That was the music playing on her sound system. "I always thought I was perfectly cast in the role of Salome. Salome had a pathologically ambitious mother named Herodias."

"Was that your mother's name?" Mrs. Wilcox asked absently.

"No, my mother's name was Vittoria. Mother was very vain about her name. Thought it very regal. I was named Aida, a slave princess." She looked toward the door. "I see,

Amedeo, that you have a guest. In a Winnebago."

"Yes," he replied. "It's Mrs. Vanderwaal. She's the mother of my godfather. She's a widow too. She retired and decided to travel around the country in a Winnebago instead of going into a home."

Mrs. Zender said, "You have never told me that you think of the Waldorf as *a home*."

William came to his rescue. "It's a retirement community."

"Yes," Mrs. Zender replied. "A retirement community."

"You will have air-conditioning," Amedeo said.

"Yes," Mrs. Zender said. "I shall have that. I'll also have housekeeping and linen service. And meal service. I shall be living in a world of paid-for incompetence, surrounded by canes, crutches, and aluminum walkers, and I shall be eating—I can hardly call it *dining*—in the company of people who discuss acid reflux and constipation as freely as they talk about the weather. I myself never talk about the weather. The temperature of any Florida day stays boringly within the age range of the inhabitants of Waldorf Court—sixty-five to ninety-nine. I shall also have complimentary transportation to the doctor and the dentist, so I shall escape the tyranny of pumping my own gas."

"Mrs. Vanderwaal pumps her own gas," Amedeo said.

A smile crept up Mrs. Zender's face. "I'm certain that Mrs. Vanderwaal is a very brave woman."

Amedeo said, "Mrs. Vanderwaal would like to come over, Mrs. Zender. There's something she would like to discuss with you."

"And is this something it takes a brave woman to do?"

"Definitely."

Mrs. Zender fluttered her hand in a dismissive gesture, and Amedeo left.

When Amedeo introduced Mrs. Zender to Mrs. Vanderwaal, Mrs. Zender said, "So you're the lady in the van?"

"Yes, I am."

"Retired?"

"Retired, yes, but spreading my wings, so to speak."

"So to speak?" Mrs. Zender said.

"My son, Peter, claims that I no sooner sprouted wings than I spread them."

"So you're fresh out of the nest?"

"Fresh out of the chrysalis."

"So you're a moth, not a butterfly?"

"You see me as I am, Mrs. Zender. Dusty wings and all."

The meeting was not going well. Mrs. Zender was not

finding Lelani Vanderwaal as humble as someone who lived in a van should be. Mrs. Wilcox immediately picked up on the tension between the two women and tried to calm the situation by offering Mrs. Vanderwaal a chair and a drink of iced tea. "Iced tea is the national drink of the South, you know."

Mrs. Zender said cuttingly, "Mrs. Wilcox still thinks of the South as a nation."

"Many people do," Mrs. Vanderwaal replied.

Amedeo looked from Mrs. Zender to Mrs. Vanderwaal and back to Mrs. Zender. Mrs. Zender was being cutting and cold because she sensed a threat. "So you've been driving through the South in your Winnebago, have you?"

Mrs. Vanderwaal took a sip of the tea before answering. "I have. I was not far from St. Malo when my son called and asked me to pay Deo a visit."

Pointing to the thick envelope in Mrs. Vanderwaal's hand, Mrs. Zender asked, "Does that have anything to do with why you stopped by?"

Amedeo answered, "Definitely."

Ever the boss, Mrs. Zender directed Amedeo and William to bring in chairs for everyone. They inadvertently set them into a semicircle as in an informal classroom or a group therapy session. Mrs. Zender pushed her seat slightly outside the orbit, giving herself almost-center stage and committing the others to being an audience. After everyone was seated, she looked briefly at the manila envelope and waited for a cue. Like a conductor ready to raise his baton, Amedeo nodded. Mrs. Zender nodded back, and she began.

"Too bad storytelling is not like opera, where many different things—singing, dancing, speaking, miming— happen simultaneously. In opera it is possible to have two people sing different parts at the same time. Like a West African griot, I shall have to dig myself out of the present, one shovel full at a time."

Obviously simmering at Mrs. Zender's high-handedness, Mrs. Vanderwaal abandoned her customary tact and corrected Mrs. Zender. "A griot's stories begin in the past and go forward. An *archeologist* begins in the present and digs into the past."

Ever the peacemaker, Mrs. Wilcox did not abandon her role. "Begin where you must, Mrs. Zender."

"Of course I shall, Mrs. Wilcox." She glanced sideways at Mrs. Vanderwaal, then focused back at center. "I must begin with my talent. I was a mezzo-soprano. I had a fine voice. Very fine. My talent was well above average. How can I explain the difference between my voice and, say, that of Maria Callas? Think of the Gulf of Mexico and the Atlantic Ocean. Both are beautiful, both come and go with tides, and both inspire dreams, but only the ocean has whales. Although mine was hardly a backwater voice, it could not sustain Moby Dick, so Mother decided that the European stage would be the best place to nourish my talent.

"Mother was right about Europe. Not only does the continent have more venues, but European standards of attractiveness are more flexible than American, and certainly less 'standard' than they were in St. Malo. Every creative endeavor must have a second section, and the first row of the second section isn't a bad place to be. I did very well there, both professionally and personally.

"I was at peace with it. I received a lot of attention. Besides, I was indulged. Daddy always supplemented my income, so I lived very well. I was happy. Mother was not. Mother was ambitious for me—as I was her product. Mother always insisted on having the immaculate best, and as long as I was in Europe, I was invisible in St. Malo, and Mother could keep the *Vindicator* informed about her diva daughter's triumphs on the continent.

"Onstage, dressed as a boy or draped as a bitch, my voice carried me through many roles. However, there came a day when the director of the opera company I was with decided that the opera *Salome* was to be done in modern dress. Salome herself was to wear a slinky red dress that he knew I could not fit into. Furthermore, this director had also decided that when Salome was to unwind the seventh veil, she was to be starkers. Well, hardly anyone wanted to see that much of me."

Mrs. Zender paused. "I'm waiting," she said. "That was a laugh line. I'm waiting for my laugh."

"Later," Mrs. Vanderwaal said coldly.

"Well," Mrs. Zender said, "she who laughs last . . ."

Mrs. Wilcox again took a cue. "Please continue, Mrs. Zender."

Mrs. Zender threw up her hands and said, "I was dismissed. Daddy was investing a lot of money into his mills to convert them from manufacturing cardboard into manufacturing wallboard for the postwar building boom, so he was not in a financial position to continue my subsidy.

"Mother knew before I did that my time on the stage was over. Most divas extend their careers by concertizing. But I could not. Being alone on stage, not playing a role, was not something I was suited for, and my name recognition was not great enough to fill a concert hall. Besides, I could not manage all that travel without people. Mother and I both knew that I would have to return to St. Malo. I had made peace with that, but Mother wanted something more. She wanted to find me something to return with—a proper accessory that would make me acceptable to St. Malo society."

Mrs. Zender stopped abruptly and stared into the middle distance. Almost intuitively, Mrs. Wilcox responded by clearing her throat, a small noise but enough to make Mrs. Zender look in her direction. With the slightest nod of her head, Mrs. Wilcox directed Mrs. Zender's attention to the large envelope, which Mrs. Vanderwaal continued to hold. She handed it over, and Mrs. Zender laid it across her lap without opening it. She ran her hand over it and looked at it for a long time before starting again. "In 1955 Vienna was in the throes of restoring itself to its former grandeur. The famous Lipizzaner horses had been saved, and the old Spanish Riding School was back in business. The Vienna Boys' Choir was singing again, and the pride of Vienna, the State Opera House, destroyed by fire during the Second World War, was to rise from its ashes."

"And this is important why?" Mrs. Vanderwaal asked.

"What I have to say about the Vienna Opera House is relevant to *The Moon Lady*. And that is why you are here, is it not, Mrs. Vanderwaal?"

"It is."

"Then you must be patient."

"Would you call waiting fifty years for an answer being patient, Mrs. Zender?"

"Yes, but I told you that I cannot tell overlapping parts at the same time like an opera. I have to tell things consecutively, because that is the way people tell stories. What I have to say about the Vienna Opera House is relevant."

"Then go on."

In a childish gesture, Mrs. Zender turned as far away as she could from Mrs. Vanderwaal without actually moving her chair. She straightened her back and continued almost defiantly.

"Back to 1955," she said. "Vienna was newly independent, and the government had adopted a policy of not hiring ex-Nazis for high-level positions. But the war had been over for ten years, and the Austrians were finding ways to accommodate men who had special talents but who may have had a questionable past. It is called *Austrian amnesia*, a term I suggest you remember.

"The State Opera House was reopened to great fanfare on November 5, 1955. The audience for the gala reopening was a specially invited international crowd. Ordinary people, the uninvited, lined up outside the opera house to watch the lucky ticket holders arrive. Like the funerals of Jacqueline Kennedy Onassis and Princess Diana, a public address system was set up so that the uninvited could hear what was going on inside. The opera was Beethoven's *Fidelio*. The conductor was Karl Böhm, a man who only seventeen years before had publicly welcomed Hitler's takeover of Austria. Everything about that evening was secondary to the one big question: Would the acoustics in the new house be as superb as they once had been? The answer was yes, they were."

"Were you there?" Amedeo asked.

"No. I was not, but Mother was."

"After her death, during one of my brief attempts to sort through and organize Mother's papers, I found the program from the gala reopening of the Vienna State Opera House. It had an elaborate, tasseled, deep blue velour cover, and inside was a list of the invited guests. Mother's name was there and so was Mr. Zender's."

Then suddenly, as if a puppet master had pulled an arm string, Mrs. Zender held up the envelope and asked Mrs. Vanderwaal, "What will I find in this envelope?"

"Papers. A photo. A handwritten memoir."

Mrs. Zender smiled knowingly and laid the envelope back down. Then, as if she were addressing a class and was asking for a show of hands, she asked, "Do any of you know about the Stockholm Syndrome?"

Only Mrs. Wilcox nodded yes—almost imperceptibly.

Without attempting to disguise the sarcasm in her voice, Mrs. Vanderwaal asked, "Is that another term you suggest we remember?"

"Yes, it is," Mrs. Zender replied. "Mother died on August 23, 1973, the very day there was a botched bank robbery in Sweden. The robbers took four people and held them hostage for six days. The hostages—three women and a man—resisted the government's efforts to help them. Even after their rescue, one of the women remained friends with the criminals. That is the incident that gave birth to the term *Stockholm Syndrome*. It has come to mean a hostage bonding with his captors." Mrs. Zender paused dramatically before continuing. "The *Stockholm Syndrome* has been used to explain Patty Hearst, members of religious cults, and battered spouses." To Mrs. Zender's credit, she did not look at Mrs. Wilcox when she said that.

"There are many ways a person can become a hostage. A captor can be a parent, a husband"—again she did not look at Mrs. Wilcox—"or it can be a social scene.

"Within two years after Mother died, Mr. Zender lost Father's business, and a hurricane named Eloise peeled back the roof over Mr. Zender's annex, took down the dock, the boathouse, and the top floor of the three-car garage, and the parties stopped. The older generation—

Mother's friends—soon found other venues, and the younger generation, the backyard barbequers/summers-in-Provence generation, never missed us. We were the Great Gatsby, after all, except that there was no green light blinking at the end of the dock. Hurricane Eloise took care of that, too.

"Mr. Zender and I continued to live here on Mandarin Road even after the money ran out. Mr. Zender adjusted his lifestyle from that of the landed gentry to that of the retired foreign diplomat. He found a silver-tipped cane somewhere in the house and started walking with a heroic limp. I think Mr. Zender made medical history as the first case on record where a cane caused a limp."

Mrs. Zender unfastened the little wing clip on the manila envelope and turned up the flap. She looked inside briefly, teasingly, but made no effort to take anything out. She laid the envelope back on her lap and folded her hands over it.

Amedeo asked, "Aren't you going to look inside? Don't you want to know—"

Mrs. Zender said, "Everyone knows that it's not over until the fat lady sings." She picked the envelope back up and pulled out the photo. She hesitated, looked at it briefly, and said, "I need my loupe. William, my loupe."

While William went to look for her magnifying glass, Mrs. Zender put on her eyeglasses and studied the picture.

Her audience was silent.

When William returned with the magnifying glass, to everyone's surprise, Mrs. Vanderwaal took it from him. Her impatience was corporeal, like a sixth person in the room. She walked—almost strutted—behind the circle of chairs until she was standing behind Mrs. Zender. Holding the loupe in her hand, she reached over Mrs. Zender's shoulder and focused on the figure on the left. "That young man," she said, jabbing at the glass, "that young man, the one on the left, is my late husband. Do you see him?" she asked. Mrs. Zender nodded. Mrs. Vanderwaal moved the magnifier ever so slightly until it was focused on the calendar on the wall. "And that is *The Moon Lady*, your wedding gift from Mr. Zender. Do you see it?" Mrs. Zender nodded again. Mrs. Vanderwaal withdrew the loupe and said, "And that, Mrs. Zender, is the fat lady we want to hear."

Mrs. Zender countered with an equal impatience, "I told you, Mrs. Vanderwaal, this isn't opera. I have to tell things one at a time."

Not even Mrs. Wilcox could discharge the current in the room, but William did. He pulled the pages of Johannes's memoir from the envelope and calmly started to read. William read fluently, allowing the pain to arrive softly from the poetry within the awkward prose. He read beyond the page where Mrs. Vanderwaal had stopped.

To me at fifteen years, that Pieter wore the Rosa Winkel *was for me both a surprise and not a surprise.*

Pieter was a homosexual, but he was much more than that. He was my brother, my parent, my guardian, my friend. As was also Klaus. My thoughts had been always the self-centered thoughts of a boy. All my thoughts were with me at the center. Everything was in relation to me. There was Pieter and me. Klaus and me. Jacob and me. Gerard and me. There were my teachers, my school, my friends and me, me, me. . . . Nothing could exist that did not have me, Johannes van der Waal, at its beginning. I never once thought about what might be between Klaus and Pieter. My brother was the shop owner and Klaus was his manager. Klaus was also my brother's roommate. I, Johannes, got along with both of them, and they got along with each other. Like everything else, there was always me in relation to them. Not them in relation to each other.

It was the Nazis who made a label for Pieter. The Nazis made a label for everyone. Besides the Yellow Stars, they had triangles of brown for Gypsies and purple for Jehovah's Witnesses. The Nazis believed that if they know

how you were born as a Jew or a Gypsy or a homosexual,
they know everything about you and can make a label for
it. But what did these labels tell you about the person who
wore them? The Nazis did not have labels for kind and
generous and brave and smart and a good friend and a
good son and a good, good, good brother.

I had known my brother, Pieter, all of my life—all
fifteen years of my life—and yet I did not know him.
I knew only the parts that I could see through my eyes
and feel in my heart. That was a lot, but the rest was like
listening in the back-back room, where from behind the
wall, you must guess at what you are seeing from what
you are hearing, and the sounds, they are muffled.

The Nazis could never make a label for Pieter van
der Waal. The Nazis knew as much about Pieter van
der Waal as the amount of him that the Rosa Winkel
covered: a small, flat Pink Triangle.

Gerard now handed to me the photograph he had
taken of me and my brother, Pieter, inside the gallery on
the night of the retirement party.

I did not cry.

I could not cry.

I think now that I did not cry because for a long time I
had been waiting for it to come—without knowing what
it was. Without knowing, I knew that the call-up would

come. I did not know that Pieter would be a Rosa Winkel, but I knew that the Nazi occupiers would find some reason to break up our family. Within me for a long time had been that fear. Maybe I did not suspect the Rosa Winkel. Maybe I thought they will take Pieter because he was helping to hide the paintings of the Rijksmuseum. Maybe I had the fear with me because since the day of the Occupation, every day, everything from eating to opening a door is marked by caution, caution, haste, haste, wait, wait. But the name of it all—caution, haste, wait—the name of it all is fear.

To Gerard, I did not speak. I could not.

I think now that I could not speak anything because there was nothing to say. To speak of my sadness was like reciting a passage that had been long ago memorized, so I did not recite the end because already I knew what it was.

All those unsaid words I could not say rose up into my throat to keep down the tears.

I looked at the photograph for a very long time. I knew that this was what I will ever see of my brother, Pieter, again.

When William laid down the pages, a swollen silence filled the room, and only then did Johannes's pain become audible.

Everyone cried.

They cried all the tears that Johannes had not.

They cried for Johannes himself, and they cried for the Dutch brother he once was and for John, the American husband and father he became. And they cried for Pieter, the *Rosa Winkel* hero they would never know.

Mrs. Zender's eye makeup streaked down her face, making punch marks like a clown.

Mrs. Wilcox found a roll of paper towels, which she passed around for everyone to use as Kleenex, and in one tender moment, Mrs. Vanderwaal reached over to Mrs. Zender, removed her glasses, and gently dabbed away the black streaks of mascara. Mrs. Zender caught Mrs. Vanderwaal's hand as she was about to remove it. "Thanks," she whispered. Mrs. Vanderwaal didn't answer.

In the hot, hushed quiet that followed, Mrs. Zender removed the two yellowed slips of paper from the envelope: the bill of sale and the exit visa. She looked at them for a long, long time.

Mrs. Vanderwaal asked—gently now—"Do you recognize that signature, Mrs. Zender?"

In a whisper, Mrs. Zender answered, "No, but I recognize the name. Karl Eisenhuth."

"What is the connection between you and Karl Eisenhuth?"

"My sound system and Mr. Zender," she replied. She straightened her back and in a subdued voice resumed her story.

"On the very day I found the souvenir program, I read in the *Vindicator* an article about the world famous acoustician, Karl Eisenhuth, having been engaged to engineer the acoustics for a new concert hall in Houston, Texas. Among Eisenhuth's credentials, the paper listed his having been on the staff of the rebuilding of the Vienna State Opera.

"Mother had tucked a clipping from the newspaper into the fold of the program saying that she had been among the glitterati as the guest of Messrs. Walter Zender and Karl Eisenhuth, the engineer who had been responsible for the resplendent qualities of the acoustics. That is when I half-teasingly suggested to Mr. Zender that he ask Eisenhuth to stop in St. Malo en route to Houston and install a sound system in our house here on Mandarin Road.

"Mr. Zender denied knowing Eisenhuth. His denial was very much like the one that had come from a real retired diplomat who was very much in the news those days.

"The retired diplomat was Kurt Waldheim, and he was in the news because he was a candidate for the presidency of Austria.

"Kurt Waldheim was a good-looking man in the gaunt,

pinched way that Austrians regard as aristocratic. He was a talented linguist—spoke several languages fluently—and had elegant manners. His lightweight intelligence and his social skills made him the perfect diplomat. However, beneath the patrician social graces beat the heart of a politician and a liar. Waldheim had capped a diplomatic career by twice being elected secretary-general of the United Nations, but when he failed to be reelected for a third term, he decided to return to his native Austria and run for its presidency.

"It was at the height of his campaign for president that reports of Waldheim's Nazi past came out. At first Waldheim claimed to have spent the last years of the war in Vienna studying law. Mr. Zender also happened to be a lawyer, and his denial of knowing Eisenhuth had strong echoes of Waldheim.

"When Waldheim was confronted with records that showed that he had not only been a Nazi officer but had participated in atrocities in the Balkans, he claimed that he could not remember something that happened so long ago. When I confronted Mr. Zender with the souvenir program and the clipping, his response was, 'I can't remember details of something as unimportant as a party.'

"Selective forgetting is the first symptom of Austrian amnesia. Remember that term?

"Then Mr. Zender turned his back to me and walked out of the room, leaning on the silver-tipped cane, his prop for his adopted role of retired foreign diplomat.

"I followed Mr. Zender. He was in the upstairs sitting room. His cane was resting across the Bibendum chair. I picked it up and sat down. I rested both hands on the cane, leaned forward like an interrogation officer, and said, 'It's time you told me what kind of a thief you really are.'

"And that is when Mr. Zender told me in all serious-ness, as if it had never been said before, that he had been a young officer, and he did not have the authority to steal. He just followed orders."

Mrs. Zender sighed. "Echoes," she said. "I was hear-ing echoes of Waldheim, for when it was revealed that Waldheim had taken an active role in deporting forty thousand Jews to Auschwitz, he said that he was just a young officer following orders."

It took a minute before Mrs. Vanderwaal said, "I am grateful that my dear husband is not around to hear this."

"I can understand that, Mrs. Vanderwaal. But do *you* want to hear it?"

Amedeo piped up, "I do," and received a volley of cold stares in return.

Mrs. Zender smiled at Amedeo. "Of course you do. I think everyone does, and oddly enough, I want to tell it, for there is an inevitability to the rest of the story. In its way it all leads to today."

Pointing to the receipt, Mrs. Zender said, "You can see that one of the things taken from the gallery was a drawing by Gustav Klimt. The rest of the story begins with that drawing."

⤷⤶

Amsterdam. 1942.

Karl Eisenhuth was a senior officer of an *Einsatzgruppen*, one of four special squads of the German Army whose responsibility it was to loot cultural treasures from the Nazi-conquered countries. *Responsibility!* It was the *responsibility* of the *Einsatzgruppen* to steal. There was an unofficial competition among these special squads to steal things that would please Hitler or Reichsmarschall Hermann Goering. Goering was notorious for his extravagant tastes. A vain, greedy man, he loved jewelry. He often wore several diamond rings on each hand and kept a pot of diamonds on his desk to play with.

Like all good Germans, Karl Eisenhuth took his looting very seriously, but stationed in Amsterdam as he was, the biggest thieves had been there before him, even before the Occupation, and the old masters that were the favorites of Hitler and Goering had already been taken.

But here and there Eisenhuth found a few objets d'art that he knew would please some of the generals, and in one small shop on Prinsengracht he found some Modern art.

Eisenhuth knew that Modern art was not allowed inside Nazi territory. If it was found, it was to be destroyed, but men like him—he certainly was not the only one—stole it anyway. They hid it to use as barter after the war if Germany lost.

The Nazis had denounced Klimt and his work as too sensual for the refined Aryans. But by 1955 Austria was independent at last, and Gustav Klimt was back in high favor. Several of his paintings were hanging in the Belevedere Palace. Modigliani was back in favor, too, but the Austrians loved Klimt more, for he was Austrian, one of their own, and he was not a Jew.

Eisenhuth was a good engineer, but at that time he certainly did not qualify by experience or reputation for a position on the acoustical staff that was rebuilding the State Opera House. But Herr Eisenhuth was ambitious, and he was clever. He took out of hiding the things he had stolen from the little shop on Prinsengracht, and persuaded one of the nouveau bureaucrats to overlook his Nazi past in exchange for one of his treasures.

The Klimt bought him a position on the technical staff. The pair of candelabra bought him a promotion.

He now had a corner office, and one day his secretary announced that a Mr. Walter Zender was there to see him. Walter Zender had been one of his lieutenants when he was in the *Einsatzgruppen*. Eisenhuth's other lieutenant had died. Poor fellow. Cause unknown.

Zender and Eisenhuth reminisced about the time they were billeted together in Amsterdam. Charming city, Amsterdam. Mr. Zender looked around Eisenhuth's office approvingly. He suggested to his former commander that with the prestige of his current position, he should be well on his way to an international clientele. Eisenhuth agreed mildly, wary of what was coming. And then, almost offhandedly, Mr. Zender said that he could never forget the time they had gone shopping at that charming gallery in Amsterdam. It was on Prinsengracht, wasn't it?

Eisenhuth knew what Zender wanted, but he stalled. He said that surely Walter Zender's postwar career had also been fortunate: He was after all an educated man—a lawyer—handsome, suave, charming, and spoke English with a Viennese tongue, which—Eisenhuth reminded him—was a compliment.

Herr Zender readily admitted his accomplishments, but what he didn't tell Eisenhuth was that although he was diligent, his colleagues did not regard him as an intellectual. Everyone recognized that his manners were beautiful—princely even—and he had learned well the art of doing favors for the right people, but he was often passed over. Success seemed always to elude him. To live the life he deserved, he needed something more. With a knowing wink, Mr. Zender told Eisenhuth that he had his eye on a wealthy American widow. A certain Mrs. Tull. Vittoria de Capua Tull was, of course, older than Mr. Zender, but a young man with an older woman was very, shall we say, "continental."

Eisenhuth told Zender that he had a drawing, a Modigliani, that he would like to give to him as a wedding gift for the widow. Zender told Eisenhuth that he accepted the drawing with thanks, but it was a little too soon to talk about weddings. He had yet to woo the woman, and the way to this widow's heart was entrée into the inner circles of European society. For that he needed two tickets to the grand opening of the rebuilt State Opera.

Eisenhuth protested. There were no tickets as such. Admission was by invitation only, and the guest list was closed. It was an international group of the rich and famous: the crowned heads of Europe, heads of state, world-famous musicians. The glitterati of the time.

Yes, Mr. Zender insisted, that was exactly the kind of company the widow liked to surround herself with. He looked around Eisenhuth's office and commented that his view was spectacular. He got up and with his hands behind his back, reminiscent of the officer Eisenhuth once was, walked to the wall where Eisenhuth's engineering certificate hung. Mr. Zender suggested that perhaps other positions he had held in the past, some other credentials so to speak, should best be forgotten.

Eisenhuth regretted having made the offer of *The Moon Lady* when he realized that what Zender really wanted was the two invitations. But he couldn't renege. His "honor" was at stake, so Mr. Zender got *The Moon Lady* and the two invitations.

When the invitation arrived, Vittoria de Capua Tull knew what they were for. She knew that Mr. Zender wanted to marry her. She was not naïve. She accepted the invitation because she had decided that she wanted Mr. Zender as well. But not for herself. She wanted Mr. Zender for her daughter. As the prince's consort, Aida Lily Tull would be lionized by St. Malo society, and her mother would become the dowager duchess. She had it all worked out. Daughter would get a husband and a Modigliani, and Mother would get a son-in-law who looked terrific in a tuxedo.

Eisenhuth got Zender's silence about his Nazi past. Vittoria Tull got Mr. Zender for her daughter. Her daughter got *The Moon Lady* as a wedding gift. The word *blackmail* never came up because by the time the negotiations were over, who could tell who was the extortionist and who, the extorted: Eisenhuth? Zender? Vittoria? Or all three?

⤸ ⤹

Mrs. Zender continued, "Mr. Zender and I got married on December 5 of the same year as the reopening of the Vienna State Opera. We had a small wedding in Venice, Mother's choice. Mother joined us in Rome, the last stop on our wedding trip, and we all flew back here to St. Malo in time for Easter. We moved into this very house on Mandarin Road, and the parties began—"

Mrs. Vanderwaal was the first to catch her breath. "Why?" she asked. "Why, *why* didn't you return *The Moon Lady* when you found out for certain that it had been Nazi loot?"

Mrs. Zender said, "I know this is going to be hard for someone like you, someone who pumps her own gas and who drives a van all over the country by herself, I know it's *very* hard for you to understand, Mrs. Vanderwaal, but the truth is, it never occurred to me. Call it the St. Malo Syndrome. I had bonded with my captor."

"Worse than that. You used *The Moon Lady* as barter to get your sound system."

"I suppose you could say that, Mrs. Vanderwaal."

"I just did."

Amedeo said, "Mrs. Zender, the first day I met you, you told me that Karl Eisenhuth installed your sound system because three words, *Aida Lily Tull*, were enough."

Mrs. Zender said, "When you consider all the baggage that comes with those three words, they were enough."

"What baggage?"

"Kurt Waldheim and Ivan the Terrible."

Mrs. Vanderwaal was aghast, and even Mrs. Wilcox was openmouthed.

It was William who asked coolly, "Why do you say that, Mrs. Zender?"

"I do read the papers, you know, and I found out that even after his Nazi past was revealed, the Austrian people elected Kurt Waldheim to be their president. His margin of victory was less than ten percent." Mrs. Zender exchanged a knowing look with Amedeo and added, "In politics even less than ten percent is enough.

"At the time there was another case about an ex-Nazi making the news. A mechanic in Cleveland, Ohio, was discovered to have been a guard at a concentration camp where he was known as Ivan the Terrible. After his Nazi past was discovered, he was stripped of his citizenship and deported. By then ex-Nazis had become so unpopular in the United States, the U.S. government declared Waldheim, the former secretary general of the United Nations, an undesirable alien and barred him from coming to America where he had once lived. Well, now, there were the two cases of two men: one who had been living in America for forty years and had been deported, and one in Austria who had been newly elected president and was not allowed back in. So there was I with my finger on two buttons.

"I pushed both.

"I suggested to Mr. Zender that he call Mr. Eisenhuth and have him reroute his trip to Houston. St. Malo would be a wonderful point of entry to America for him. If he tried to come in through any other port, his name could mysteriously appear on a list of ex-Nazis, and he could possibly have trouble getting in.

"So Herr Eisenhuth entered the United States through the port of St. Malo, designed my system, paid for all the materials, and supervised its installation. After he left I put *The Moon Lady* away. Tucked it into a corner of the library. I couldn't destroy it. It is lovely, isn't it? But I never displayed it or enjoyed it."

Mrs. Vanderwaal was dumbfounded. "You consider that penance? Never enjoying it? Or were you really just protecting yourself and your stolen goods?"

"I hardly came into the library. I more or less forgot about it until I had to move. Then I knew it would be discovered."

William asked, "Were you counting on Amedeo to do that?"

"Not at first. When I hired Mrs. Wilcox, I knew she had discovered the Chinese silk screen. I do read the papers, you know. But then Amedeo came along."

"You knew I wanted to discover something, didn't you?"

"Yes. I had heard you say that you wanted to find something that had been lost that no one knew had been lost until you found it. I thought that with your name being the same as Modigliani's and your being Jewish and Italian, there was enough there to pique your interest."

"You planted it, didn't you?"

"Of course I did. I planted it when I found out that you were going to an exhibit of Degenerate art. The day you recited that little poem about Modigliani, I was sure you would turn *The Moon Lady* over to that person in Sheboygan—"

"Are you referring to my son? Is he 'that person in Sheboygan'?"

"If he is the person who put together that show of Degenerate art."

"He is."

"Then he's that person in Sheboygan."

"That person in Sheboygan has a name, Mrs. Zender. His name is Peter. Peter Vanderwaal. He is named for Johannes's brother, Pieter. Johannes's brother, parent, guardian, friend. I think you should remember it, Mrs. Zender, because his name is relevant as all memorials are relevant. Say his name, Mrs. Zender. Say Peter Vanderwaal."

Mrs. Zender repeated, "Peter Vanderwaal."

Momentarily satisfied, the two women turned from each other.

Then Mrs. Vanderwaal scolded, "You, Mrs. Zender, didn't want Amedeo to save *The Moon Lady*, you wanted him to relieve you of owning stolen merchandise that you yourself had done nothing about for half your life."

"I haven't had my sound system for that long—half my life."

"But you did nothing. Nothing! You obviously read the papers, Mrs. Zender. You know that even museums have had to give back stolen works—works that have been hanging on their walls for years. There are laws, Mrs. Zender."

Worried that this exchange would escalate into warfare, Mrs. Wilcox asked, "When you planted that picture, Mrs.

Zender, did you have any idea that Amedeo would have a personal connection to it?"

"How could I know that? Didn't you just hear Mrs. Vanderwaal need to remind me of the name Peter? Peter Vanderwaal didn't enter into my plans until I found out he was sponsoring an exhibit of Degenerate art."

William asked, "Were Bert and Ray unexpected?"

Mrs. Zender's reply was vague. "I guess I should have paid more attention to Mrs. Wilcox's lists. But I didn't. I simply found myself sitting in the music room with *The Moon Lady* perched on the piano." And then, as if a ventriloquist had entered the room, Mrs. Zender launched into a wicked imitation of Bert: "'What do you think, Ray? Do you think we'll be arrested for dealing in pornography if we display this in our shop?'" Mrs. Zender paused briefly before continuing with an accurate but mean impersonation of Ray. "'If it's old enough and expensive enough, it's not pornographic, it's antique.'" Slipping back into her normal conversation tone, she added, "Those two men had no more intention of displaying *The Moon Lady* in their shop than they had of running with the bulls in Pamplona."

Amedeo listened with his heart in his throat. Mrs. Zender was being carried away by her performance, and she couldn't stop. Gone was the mild, mocking tone that he was accustomed to hearing. He didn't like Bert and Ray. They were jealous of Mrs. Wilcox, but they were not mean. The look on William's face told him that the acid in Mrs. Zender's voice had etched him, too.

Mrs. Zender softened her tone and continued, "Bert and Ray were going to march Modigliani straight to the nearest museum and make a profit that would put Mrs. Wilcox's sale to the Freer in the shade. However, I also knew, as they obviously did not, that no museum would buy it." She looked at Mrs. Vanderwaal. "Yes, I do read the papers." She turned back to her audience and added, "But by then Amedeo had allowed things to go too far."

Amedeo was incensed. "How did *I* let things go too far? You're accusing me of not doing a job you never gave me. Like the telephones. You let me guess at what you want and then you accuse me . . ." Amedeo opened his mouth to say something more, but nothing would come out.

Mrs. Zender purred. "Admit it, Amedeo. It wasn't until I walked out that you realized what a disaster it would be if Bert and Ray bought *The Moon Lady*."

"Did you play me, Mrs. Zender? Did you play me the way you played Mr. Zender—like a harpsichord?"

"Never! I could never play you like a harpsichord,

Amedeo. You are too *fortissimo*, but I didn't need to. Bert or Ray—one of them—had already plucked a G-string." And then, like the mimic she was, Mrs. Zender slipped into Ray's voice. "Moe-DIG-lee-ahn-nee . . ."

And then suddenly Mrs. Wilcox jumped to her feet and clapped her hands.

Amedeo jumped. What was happening? Mrs. Wilcox was acting out of character, and so was Mrs. Vanderwaal. They were the peacemakers, and now they were calling attention to themselves the way that Mrs. Zender did.

"Let us just think about Bert and Ray for a minute. Think about why wouldn't they want a signed drawing? The price was right. Mrs. Zender had even approved it. But now think about what would have happened if Amedeo had not stopped it." She looked around the room. "Mrs. Zender's already given us all a hint about that. We already know that no museum is gonna buy anything unless'n they investigate it. They call it *vetting*. And when the vetting is done, and they find out that there drawing don't have a proper provenance, there's gonna be one right big fuss. And that is when Bert and Ray will be enraged, and rightfully so. They're gonna call the newspaper. And rightfully so. And the paper will print an article. And prob'ly put it on a wire service. Such things make the national news these days. There would be martyrs, namely

Bert and Ray. And why wouldn't they be? They were sold stolen merchandise, and William and me would be caught in the middle of selling it. Something I should'na done. But I didn't follow up as I shoulda. I suspected something about *The Moon Lady* but I never suspected that it had cost a boy his life."

Mrs. Zender said, "You could say that *The Moon Lady* saved a boy's life."

Mrs. Vanderwaal was enraged. "How can you say that?"

Mrs. Zender held up the exit visa. "This saved a life."

Amedeo looked at Mrs. Zender. She lifted her chin and was smiling as she had done the day of her mock dinner party. She was giving a performance.

Mrs. Vanderwaal was seething. She said, "I don't think, Mrs. Zender, that you can possibly call Eisenhuth or Zender a hero. And *you*, Mrs. Zender, do not get to choose." She folded her arms across her chest; so tightly that Amedeo thought she would fall apart if she let go.

Amedeo looked from one to the other: the prosecutor and the defendant. One lived her life as an executive, and the other as an artist. Like his mother and Jake, he loved them both. Would he have to choose? Or could they share custody?

William conferred briefly with the angel on his shoulder, then he took his mother by the elbow and gently nudged her forward until she was standing between the two women facing them both.

Mrs. Wilcox spoke slowly. "You might could say that, Mrs. Zender. You might say that *The Moon Lady* saved a young boy's life, but I wouldn't recommend you sayin' that. Not in public anyways. Over to the Waldorf, there's a lot of them cane-and-crutch crowd that's not gonna see it that way at all. They're all old, but most of them has nothin' wrong with their long-term memories, and when they read about how that picture come to St. Malo, they're gonna see it as having *cost* lives, and—much as I know about them—I reckon they're not gonna want to have much to do with someone who was once married to a . . . a . . . foreign person such as Mr. Zender once was."

Mrs. Vanderwaal said, "The fat lady is finished."

Looking from *The Moon Lady* to Mrs. Zender and back, Amedeo asked, "Which fat lady?"

"Depends," Mrs. Zender said. "Which one of us do you want to see naked, not nude?"

There followed a moment as charged as Macy's at Christmas.

Mrs. Wilcox cleared her throat. "I done some reading, and I found out there's a committee up there in Washington that's set up to investigate claims to restore art stolen by the Nazis to the rightful owners. Mrs. Vanderwaal could contact them, or . . ." Mrs. Wilcox stopped and cleared her throat again. "Or Mrs. Zender could return *The Moon Lady* to the widow of the inheritor . . . or Mrs. Vanderwaal and Mrs. Zender could both take some time to sit down together and make a choice."

Mrs. Wilcox sat down.

Mrs. Zender turned to Mrs. Vanderwaal, and they turned away from their anger, and then they turned toward each other and made a choice.

20

It was winter, and it was Wisconsin. Peter Vanderwaal, Mrs. Vanderwaal, Mrs. Wilcox, William, Mrs. Zender, and Amedeo Kaplan stood—freezing—on the loading dock of the Sheboygan Art Center. They were variously bundled up, but it was stabbing cold.

Amedeo had raided the carton of winter clothes that he had not opened since he had moved to St. Malo. He had found a hooded jacket for himself and another— a little short in the sleeves—for William. Mrs. Wilcox was wearing a pair of his mother's boots and one of his mother's coats—a little long in the sleeves—that Amedeo had insisted she borrow. Mrs. Wilcox didn't complain, but Amedeo knew she was cold; her nose was red and her eyes were tearing, but she was smiling. Mrs. Zender was in a full-length fox fur. The shoulders of her coat were so wide that anyone who did not know her might think she had forgotten to remove the hanger before putting it on. She wore white leather gloves up to her elbow, which had yellowed with age and stiffened with cold, and her fur hat—as wide as a medium pizza—posed a serious rival to Peter's *pelzkeppe*.

Peter was wearing fur-lined gloves and a bespoke shearling coat that brushed the ankles of his riding boots. He was not cold, but the cold gave him an excuse to stamp his feet. In truth, he could not keep still. Today was the day they were to deliver both of his new acquisitions for the gallery. As the truck backed up, Peter could already picture them on the wall in the front gallery: the oil painting in its simple, simply beautiful new frame (which he had selected), and the drawing in its original restored frame. He took off one glove so that he could finger the two brass plates he had in his pocket. One said:

AMEDEO MODIGLIANI

1884–1920

The Moon Lady

Crayon on Paper

GIFT OF JOHN AND LELANI VANDERWAAL

IN MEMORY OF PIETER VAN DER WAAL

The other brass plate said:

HENRI MATISSE

1869–1954

Paysage à L'Estaque

Oil on Canvas

MUSEUM PURCHASE

ANONYMOUS DONOR

Peter served his impatience by mentally writing his opening statement for the speech he would give at the paintings' unveiling. Matisse's *Landscape at L'Estaque* had a sky that was green and a pasture that was blue, so he could very well begin his remarks by saying, "Works by Amedeo Modigliani and Henri Matisse were once forbidden." No, he thought, these works deserve a different beginning.

As the truck backed up, Amedeo watched the three women: Mrs. Zender, Mrs. Vanderwaal, and Mrs. Wilcox. And he thought about the ten percent and the ninety percent.

And he thought: Suppose you find a tusk and have a woolly mammoth named after you, or you find America and have the capital of Ohio named after you, or you invent a process and have pasteurization named after you;

you have to give up some part of that invisible ninety percent. And suppose you find a friend, a real friend; then, too, you have to give up some of that ninety percent.

William was standing on the loading platform with his hands deep inside his pockets.

Amedeo watched as he tipped the hood of his anorak to the angel on his shoulder. And even though William was his best friend in the world, and even if he was William's best friend as well, he would never know what thoughts William sent to that angel on his shoulder, because that angel was part of his ninety percent that had to stay anonymous.

Then he thought about Pieter and Peter and Johannes and John. And he thought about the three words *Aida Lily Tull.*

And he thought about the edge between the ninety percent and the ten percent.

Sometimes that edge was cunning, and sometimes it was kind. Sometimes it was shabby. And sometimes it was heroic.

But it was always mysterious.

Definitely.

acknowledgments

to my **friends** and **colleagues**—
  at **simon & schuster**: beth sue **rose**, emma **dryden**,
      rubin **pfeffer**, and rick **richter** for their enthusiasm;
  at **aladdin**: ellen **krieger** for always making it a special
      pleasure to meet with her approval;
  at **home**: theresa **dinuzzo** for her italian lyricism;
  at **atheneum**: jeannie **ng** for her scrutiny and patience
      with missed deadlines; jordan **brown** for his
      heroic keyboarding; **&** russell **gordon** for his
      panache and his energy and for making this book
      the focus of both; **&** ginee **seo** for the joy of
      sharing her luminous mind and hard black pencils
you are/have become/will always be **the home team**
and have my **thanks forever**.

DATE DUE

OCT 1 2 2016	
	PRINTED IN U.S.A.